DAGGER'S EDGE

L. L. RICHMAN
DAGGER'S
EDGE

THE BIOGENESIS WAR • BOOK 4

DAGGER'S EDGE

L. L. RICHMAN

DELTA V PRESS

This is for you, my readers.

Thank you for waiting four long years to get to the end.

ABOUT THE BIOGENESIS WAR™ UNIVERSE

Humanity has reached the stars.

With colonies established throughout the Sol System, explorers hungry for new ventures traveled beyond its borders to colonize nearby Alpha Centauri.

At the same time, a brave pair of ships set their sights a bit farther afield—on the binary stars Procyon and Sirius. Those who settled there called themselves the Geminate Alliance.

Such distances made interaction prohibitive. Even with the Scharnhorst drive's ability to triple the speed of light, travel between the colonies was measured in months, if not years.

In the mid-twenty-fifth century, that all changed. The Geminate Alliance stunned the known worlds with the invention of the Calabi-Yau Gate. The gates folded space, enabling instantaneous travel between star systems. True interstellar commerce became a reality.

In general, humanity prospered, but it wasn't perfect. In certain pockets within the settled worlds, organized crime carved out a foothold. Free speech allowed dissenters a voice, yet some weren't content with the results that came from such a platform. In other places, dictators flourished.

Then one man committed a crime so heinous, it united all the star nations. Putting aside their squabbles, they came together to bring him to justice. Yet at the eleventh hour, he slipped through their fingers, never to be heard from again.

One person refused to give up the hunt. But this one cannot do it alone. The mission requires the service and sacrifice of another.

Someone willing to go to hell and back to bring Asher Dent to justice.

ALSO BY LL RICHMAN

For updates on upcoming titles see https://www.llrichman.com

The Biogenesis War

The Chiral Agent, June 2020

The Chiral Protocol, September 2020

Chiral Justice, February 2021

Dagger's Edge, September 2024

The Biogenesis War Files: The Early Years

Operation Cobalt, December 2020

Ambush in the Sargon Straits, June 2020

The Chiral Conspiracy, June 2020

Sudden Death, August 2021

Vision Rising

Vision Rising, May 2023

Vision's Gambit, June 2023

Vision's Pawn, July 2023

Battlefield Diplomacy

Battlefield Diplomacy, Winter 2024

Lost Colony, Winter 2024

Insurrection, Early 2025

RIFT (A Near-Future Technothriller)

Rift, Early 2025

Splintered, Mid 2025

Enfield Genesis

Alpha Centauri: Rise of the Kentaurus AIs, 2018

Proxima Centauri: Hunt for the Lost AIs, 2018

Tau Ceti: The Phage, 2018

Epsilon Eridani: Crisis in the Little River, 2019

Sirius: Flight of the Hyperion, 2019

The Sol Dissolution Series (with M. D. Cooper)

Venusian Uprising, 2019

Assault on Sedna, 2020

Hyperion War, 2020

The Fall of Terra, 2021

CONTENTS

"The best weapon against an enemy is another enemy."

~ Friedrich Nietzsche

ONE:
UNEXPECTED ENCOUNTER

Humboldt Space Elevator
St. Clair Township, Ceriba
Geminate Alliance (Procyon System)

The cabin of the space elevator came to a full stop as it touched down on the surface. A green light flashed, and the elevator's SI announced. "Welcome to St. Clair Township, capital of Ceriba. Please be careful when retrieving your belongings, as they may have shifted during our descent. Enjoy your stay."

Elodie Cyr unwebbed and reached beneath her seat for the carrier that had indeed shifted, though entirely on its own. Small paws shoved against the carrier's soft, screened sides as she hefted its strap over her shoulder and stood, waiting patiently for the passengers in front of her to disembark.

Her own passenger wasn't nearly as patient—or as quiet. *{No likey. Lemme out! Lemme out! I be good.}*

Ell resisted the urge to laugh at the mental voice that had popped into her head, courtesy of the evanescent wire embedded in her brain. *{Uh huh. Remember what you did the last time one of* *us fell for that line? Thad had to shell out a lot of credits to cover the trinkets you stole from that woman's craft booth.}*

The ferret inside the carrier chittered. *{Was shiny.}*

Like that was an excuse.

The line started moving and Ell slipped into the flow. Once inside the station proper, her gaze immediately went high, drawn out of habit to areas within the spaceport that would make a good sniper's hide.

Old habits died hard. Ell quashed the thought the moment it floated to the front of her mind because in truth, it wasn't accurate. Good training died hard, especially those seared into the gray matter of one's brain by the two Ds—discipline and drill instructors.

But Ell's days as a special forces sniper were over. Her hand reached for the point above her knee where surgeons had attached a bioidentical leg. The original had been mangled beyond repair.

Though Ell had a clear memory of events leading up to the explosion, everything that followed was fuzzy. They'd been on a covert extraction deep in Alpha Centauri's Sargon Straits. The mission was a success, all packages accounted for, but the timing had been rushed. All indicators pointed to things heating up, but nothing had suggested a coup. But apparently, the Akkadians hadn't read the same memo.

Damn Akkadians.

Things had hit a flashpoint just as they'd hustled the Geminate Consulate out the back door. Ell had gone high to cover their six, so she was last to retreat. An Akkadian assault ship had hit the airlock right as Ell entered it.

From that point on, all she had were vague impressions. Shouting. Rough hands pulling her inside the ship. Hard acceleration. Shock and pain and then blessed numbness as their medic knocked her out. She'd awakened with a leg that wasn't her own. A different kind of pain was now her constant companion, every moment of every day.

The complex network of artificial nerve fibers grafted into her own nervous system were made of the same SmartCarbyne that formed her military endoskeleton, which had never given her any trouble. But the protective shell that reinforced bone, organs, and sinew during high delta-*v* maneuvers was made to protect parts of her body. These artificial nerves *replaced* them.

Unfortunately, she was one of a rare handful of people whose bodies did not respond well to the transplant. In Ell, they caused a painful feedback loop, a transient neuropathy that never truly went away. She'd been to the best surgeons in the Alliance; every attempt to resolve the issue had failed.

Had it been just the pain, she might have found a way to gut it out, but the carbyne nerves had a funny way of dropping signal strength without warning, causing her leg to collapse. That meant that Ell-the-sniper was a liability to the Special Reconnaissance Unit where she served.

It had been a devastating blow. Being an SRU sniper wasn't just Ell's career; it was her life, her identity. But a certain someone wouldn't allow her to just give up. And damn it, she was too used to following whatever orders Captain Thad Severance gave to fight him. So, when a 'friend from the NCIC' showed up and offered Ell a job as a special agent, she knew better than to turn it down.

Naval Criminal Investigation Command might not be sexy or glamorous like the special forces, but it would pay the bills.

She'd soon come to realize that the skills she'd mastered as a sniper applied here, too. Keen observation, the ability to blend in with her surroundings, situational awareness, and intense focus were just a few of the traits she'd mastered as a sniper that carried over to her new position.

Then a recent case had turned everything on its ear. Ell was in the game once again—and she was back with her old unit. More accurately, she'd been pulled into a conspiracy that spanned all inhabited space, and them along with her.

Ell shoved the memories aside, annoyed that she'd allowed her thoughts to wander when she should have been monitoring her surroundings. She gave the area a good scan, her head on a practiced swivel just casual enough to not look studied.

Everything was as it should be. The area was filled with passengers coming and going, some running to catch connecting flights, others busy corralling excitable kids or heading for baggage claim.

The only baggage Ell had was tucked into an inside pocket of the ferret's carrier. Unlike many around her, this trip was routine, part of Ell's standard commute.

Ordinarily, she wouldn't be taking work home, but the intel she'd just been given had piqued her interest. She'd wanted more time to study it, but Quinn had gone into mother hen mode and shamed her into going home 'at a decent hour for once.'

That was when she'd found out he'd volunteered her to babysit the furry little pickpocket slung over her shoulder. She'd tried to get out of it, but her words had fallen on deaf ears.

On a resigned sigh, Ell exited the spaceport. It was a perfect spring day, the sky a brilliant blue and the breeze soft on her exposed arms. The carrier lurched, causing her to widen her stance to stay balanced.

{Ooo pretty. Wanna climb!}

She didn't have to look to know what the ferret had seen. A new art installation by one of Ceriba's premiere sculptors had recently been added to the spaceport's grounds. Ornate brushed silver swept elegantly aloft, as if the sculpture's two abstract arms were trying to touch the sky. And yes, it was shiny.

{This, right here, is why you're in a carrier,} she scolded mentally, flagging down the nearest air taxi. *{If I let you out, I'd never see you again. And that would break Sam's heart.}*

{Sam-Sam, nice doctor. No make her sad.}

{Then behave,} she said as an autonomous aircar stopped in front of her.

Half an hour later, the vehicle started its descent. Ell's destination was Montpelier, a suburb south of the city. Its trendy retail district was a few blocks from Ell's townhouse, and home to Ceriba's famous Restaurant Row.

The cab touched down, and its fee popped up on her evanescent wire. Ell transferred the credits over and exited the vehicle, accompanied by the excited chittering of a ferret ready to explore new places.

"Just hang tight a little longer. I need to grab both of us something to eat, and then we'll head home."

The smells wafting her way made her stomach grumble. A boulangerie was up ahead, and Ell knew from experience that it also had a nice assortment of meats and cheeses to go with its fresh-every-morning croissants. She headed for it at a brisk walk.

Ell was halfway there when the itching sensation of someone watching hit her hard. She glanced casually around, checking faces, window reflections, shadows in unexpected areas, anything that might indicate a malicious presence. She found nothing.

The owner of the boulangerie was an acquaintance; he nodded cheerfully at her as she entered. Normally, she would linger over the wealth of choices. Not today.

She grabbed food quickly and paid over her wire, then waited for the counter to clear before approaching the proprietor.

"Would you mind terribly if I used the facilities?" she asked in a low tone.

The boulangerie had one of those 'no public restrooms' holosigns posted out front, but the owner had been there the night a man had been killed outside his shop. He'd seen Ell racing toward the threat, not away from it. And he'd never forgotten.

"Of course. It's in the back."

"Thanks, Bruce." She gave him a brief smile, then slipped down the corridor… and out the back door.

Her SDR was complex enough that it should have caught anyone shadowing her—but at the end of the surveillance detection route, she came up empty. There was no one there, yet the feeling persisted.

The townhouse was in an upscale neighborhood with good security; the street was tidy and well lit. It made it hard to keep to the shadows. Still, she figured she'd be just fine as long as no nosy neighbors came out to ask why she was skulking around in their bushes.

When she slipped inside her foyer, Ell set the carrier down, drew her weapon, and cleared each room. By the time she was done, she had begun to feel a little foolish. There was literally nothing to indicate she was being watched or followed.

Ell holstered her pistol and backtracked to retrieve the carrier. "Maybe Quinn's right. Maybe I do need a vacation," she muttered.

She stepped into the foyer and froze. There, standing over the ferret's carrier, was an Akkadian assassin.

TWO:
OLD ACQUAINTANCES

Townhome
Montpelier, Ceriba

Ell shifted into a stance that would allow her to respond to any move from the Akkadian but made no aggressive moves—yet.

The assassin's bronzed skin and brown braids blended almost seamlessly into the foyer's coffee-colored walls. There was only the barest flash of color, beads woven into the braids, that caught the light at the turn of a head.

Ell tensed, recalling what Quinn had told her about those. *One bead, one kill.*

And then the assassin spoke. "I didn't think you had a pet."

The words were husky, spoken with an accent some might consider exotic.

"I don't, unless you count begonias."

"The one in the kitchen needs watering."

"They like it dry."

The assassin laughed. It sounded like genuine amusement, but with the Dagger, you never could tell.

"It is good to see you again, *zhídé de duìshǒu.*"

Zhídé de duìshǒu. Worthy opponent.

"I'd like to say the same, Dacina, but…" Ell let out an exasperated breath and relaxed her stance. "What the hell are you doing here on Ceriba? And why didn't you go through channels?"

Dacina's brow rose at that, and Ell realized two things—one, her comment had been pretty stupid, and two, Dacina never had been a woman of many words.

Funny, because most folks said the same thing about Ell. She wasn't entirely comfortable drawing that comparison, either.

"Okay, fine, I know. Even though our countries are no longer on a war footing, it's not like they'd let you come down and say hello." Ell wrestled briefly with the thought of inviting Dacina in. She'd clearly been through the residence, so what would it hurt to formalize it. "Come on in. I see you've met Snotface."

"Yes. He is… talkative. But Snotface?" Dacina lifted the carrier and stepped forward, transferring it to Ell's outstretched hand.

"I didn't name him. He came that way. And yeah, he's talkative. Sam thinks it's because he was born deaf. When they implanted a wire, well… the experience was so novel, he went overboard. Or maybe it's just because he's a ferret. Who knows?"

She unsealed the carrier and lifted the ferret up until they were nose to nose. "You behave, you hear me? No hoarding shiny objects. If you see something you like, you bring it to me and *ask* first. Understood?"

The ferret blinked and washed his whiskers with one paw. *{See shiny, bring to Ell, yes yes.}*

That felt too easy, but Ell's experience with the pair of ferrets, usually housed at the orbital base or the military research facility nearby, was sketchy at best. "Okay then. Your food and water will be in the kitchen." She set him down and he scampered out of sight.

"Is that the chiral one?" Dacina asked from behind her.

Ell pivoted to face her…

Her what? Adversary? Partner? Her co-conspirator on their last mission?

"No, Sneaky Pete's with Sam. The chiral animals never leave her care."

"Doctor Travis is well. And her captain, too."

Those didn't sound like questions. Ell wondered if that meant the Geminate Alliance still had intel leaks they needed to plug.

"They are," she replied, not seeing the harm in giving that much away. She headed into the kitchen, wondering if she should notify Thad and the others about Dacina, then decided against it. The assassin would surely pick up her transmission. She wouldn't know what was being sent, but the active comm signal would be a dead giveaway. She'd be doing the same if their positions were reversed.

Ell gestured to a bar stool at the kitchen island, then walked around to the other side where she'd left her food purchase on the counter. Thankfully, she'd bought enough to feed both herself and her unexpected guest. "Have a seat. How is your general these days?"

Dacina glided over to the chair and sat in it, the dagger in her hand materializing as if by magic. She set it ceremonially on the stone surface between them, pointy end sideways. It had to be some sort of Akkadian ritual. She made a mental note to ask Quinn; he would know.

What Ell *did* know was that General Che Josza's Fierce Dagger was a woman not to be underestimated—ever.

"The general is well. He and the Premier have worked hard to root out the traitors within the government. Those loyal to Asher Dent."

Ell repressed a shudder at mention of that name. Asher Dent was the mastermind of the conspiracy she'd been sucked into. His plan—to take control of every Coalition nation with the help of the traitor Clint Janus—had nearly succeeded.

Janus, a neurobiologist, had been a civilian contractor working for the Geminate Navy. He'd stolen chiral material from an interdicted planet and used it to clone chiral copies of world leaders for Dent's use.

Ell, and the woman seated across from her, had been instrumental in taking them both down.

Skittering sounds announced Snotface's arrival, reminding Ell that not *all* of the chiral clones had been created on Janus's watch. Some of them—the viable ones—had been made earlier. And without anyone's permission.

{Lookee! Sparkle-jingly thingies! I keep?}

It did not escape Ell's notice that the question was directed at Dacina, not her. "Careful, he's a shyster. That one will try to con you out of your last credit."

Dacina looked down at the ferret, who had stretched himself to his full length to reach her lap. In one paw was a set of credit chits that belonged, no doubt, to the owner from whom Ell was leasing the unit.

"He is still entangled with his clone, mentally? They communicate well?"

"That's classified. By your government as well as mine."

The assassin favored her with a look that told Ell to stop wasting her time.

"Yes, they are still connected at the quantum level. And not like Janus's clones. Snotface could get hurt and it wouldn't affect his chiral twin."

{You no pay attention! Me me me me! Lookee, lookee!} the ferret insisted, shaking the shiny silver pieces in his paw.

"What made your scientist think installing evanescent wires inside their brains was a good idea?" Dacina asked, taking the proffered credit chits and placing them on the counter.

Ell had wondered the same thing many a time. "I have no idea. The hunting cats are better than the ferrets. These guys take some getting used to, but they're sweet. And usually well-behaved."

She nearly choked when Snotface used the assassin as a makeshift ladder, swarming up her leg to gain access to the countertop.

Dacina lifted a single brow. "You were saying?"

"Snotface! Off the counter, now!"

The animal gave her a guileless look then scampered down the same way he'd come up.

Ell shook her head and ordered the kitchen's SI to sanitize the surface. The Synthetic Intelligence chimed once to acknowledge, then chimed again to signal the sterilization was complete.

"Quick, while he's gone…" She lifted the bag of croissants and gave Dacina a questioning look. When the assassin nodded, Ell retrieved a bread knife and went to work, slicing the fluffy, buttery concoctions and filling them with layers of meat and cheese.

"You didn't travel nearly a dozen light-years just to check up on our chiral clones," she said, sliding a plate across to Dacina. "So, why did you come?"

Dacina fingered the sandwich, then pushed the plate deliberately aside and looked up at Ell.

And then Ell knew. She *knew*.

"I have located Asher Dent."

THREE:
MISSION PARAMETERS

Joint Operations Command Headquarters
Parliament Hill
St. Clair Township, Ceriba

Thad Severance paced the confines of the building's lobby, worry for Ell increasing every time an aircar passed and didn't stop.

"Relax, she's fine. She'll be here soon," Micah said from his position by the front entrance. His tone was relaxed, but his stance showed he was on alert.

"Don't you be telling me to relax, hoss. Last time she was around the Dagger, Dacina *shot* her."

"With Ell's permission. To take down the guy holding a gun to *her* head. So relax, she's a friendly. Sort of."

Thad jabbed an accusing finger in Micah's direction. "Don't forget, I was there when those *couyon* kidnapped Sam. I remember exactly how 'relaxed' you were then."

The Shadow Recon pilot held up his hands. "You got me there. But I feel like I should point out, we've got Boone and Asha up on the roof with P-SCARs. And Jonathan and Katie are flying cover. Dacina's not going to hurt your girl."

Thad grunted, annoyed that Micah was right. Not that it helped. Then a hand landed on Thad's shoulder and squeezed. Thad knew without turning who it belonged to—Gabriel Alvarez, the man he'd gone through the selection Q-course with, and the NCIC agent who had given an injured Ell purpose when she needed to find her way.

"Don't sell her short. She can handle herself," Gabe reminded him. "Besides, she and Dacina have a connection. Dacina sought her out for a reason."

"That's what's worrying me, *ami*," Thad said. "I don't want some beaded-and-braided assassin pulling her into some Akkadian op without backup."

"They're coming here, aren't they?" Gabe countered mildly. The look on his face told Thad that he was being just a bit irrational about the whole thing.

"What can I say? Where Ell's concerned, my judgement's all shot to hell."

"No, it's not," Micah said. "You're just hyperaware of anything that might harm her, and that's a good thing, as long as you can keep it in check."

Unaccountably, his words struck Thad as funny. He lifted a brow. "You lecturin' *me* about keeping a cool head, Navy?"

"Ah, shove it, Severance." Micah straightened, his eyes growing distant as he listened to something no other living being could hear—a quantumly entangled mental connection that he and his chiral twin shared. "Okay, Jonathan's spotted them. They're in an air taxi, two blocks out and headed this way." He grinned. "They have Snotface with them. If that doesn't say 'I come in peace,' nothing does."

"Damn ferret."

Crisp footsteps sounded behind him. "What happened to 'damn cat'?" Colonel Valenti asked dryly as she stopped beside him.

"I'd be feeling a lot better about things if a fifty-kilo hunting cat were riding shotgun with her instead of Snotface," he said. "Ferrets aren't exactly apex predators."

His commanding officer made a sound that could have been agreement, or not. Her gaze was fixed outside. "Here they come."

The aircar pulled as close to the entrance as was possible, so it was hidden by the protective overhang. Ell made a hand sign to Micah, who triggered the doors; when they slid open, she and her companion dashed from the car into the lobby. If they'd done their job well, it would be enough to keep any unwanted surveillance from spotting the foreign visitor.

"This way," Valenti ordered, ushering them into a waiting lift.

They exited onto a secured subterranean level. Valenti led them down the hall, stopping outside a room that was clearly a SCIF. The sensitive, compartmented information facility would guarantee complete isolation for their talk. That meant nothing in, nothing out.

A guard stood beside a row of shelves that held Faraday containers with biolocks that could be personalized. Thad went first, sliding his everyday carry handgun into one of the boxes, along with his knife and the backup comms device he kept stashed in a cargo pocket. Dacina stepped up next, her willingness to divest herself of a significant personal arsenal a clear, albeit nonverbal, declaration of intent.

The process repeated itself with Micah, Ell, even Valenti. If the guard was surprised that one of Ell's 'devices' was a ferret, it didn't show. He simply took the carrier, promising to route Snotface back to Sam as soon as possible.

Once everyone was inside and the door had shut, Thad felt the familiar sensation of his wire implant being cut off. It was standard SCIF protocol.

Valenti got straight to the point. "Dacina Zian. Agent Cyr says you have located Asher Dent. Why are you here, then, and not out apprehending him?"

Dacina's lip may have curled just the least bit. It was hard for

Thad to tell; the Akkadian was known for her stoicism. "Because war is art. And because there is a poetic symmetry to your inclusion. Janus twisted your discovery into a curse. Asher Dent weaponized it, using it against both your people and mine. Together, we shall take him down."

Gabe's knee nudged Thad under the table. The physical contact initiated a peer-to-peer connection. *{Is it just me or did I catch a whiff of bullshit there? Akkadian assassins don't have partners. They prefer to operate solo. Unless she actually **likes** working with us but is too proud to admit it.}*

{You're the profiler. You tell me.}

Gabe fell silent, assessing. *{Yeah,}* he said after a moment. *{She likes working with us. We made a great team before. And we're united in this cause. We all want Dent to stand before the Coalition tribunal, to answer for his sins.}*

{Speak for yourself, hoss. I want to pound his sorry ass into the ground. Take him apart and bury the pieces in the four corners of the known universe for what he did.}

{You know,} Gabe said, *{that might be why she came to us. Think about how many people want a piece of Dent. He had their Premier, Rin Zhou imprisoned. Jiu Liam, the president of An-Yang, very nearly escaped being cloned. Our own Prime Minister, who **was** cloned.}*

Thad grunted his agreement. *{What's your point, hoss?}*

{Too many cooks in the kitchen. With us, it's contained. Small mission unit, surgical strike. In and out.} Gabe paused. *{And if he fires first, it would be a clear case of self-defense.}*

{I like the way you think, ami.} Thad turned his attention back to the conversation in time to hear Valenti ask Dacina where Dent was hiding.

"He has a compound in the Lantern city of Illuminari."

"On Venus, huh?" Thad said. "Interesting."

Illuminari was old, dating back to the earliest days of space colonization. It was one of five floating cities that had been built in the cloud deck—sixty kilometers above the planet's surface, where temperature and pressure were the same as on Earth.

The atmosphere was another matter—it was a billion times more acidic than anything found back home. Each city was encased in an electrostatic shield, a protective bubble filled with breathable air.

"The compound is vast, built with funds siphoned from the Akkadian treasury reserve. It is on the lower level, where certain business transactions are known to take place, and few questions are asked."

"Ahh." Valenti's reaction indicated there was more to Dacina's explanation than met the eye. "The Gaming District. That makes sense. He'd be right at home there."

"Yes. He provides distribution services for illegal substances."

Thad knew Dacina well enough to pick up the anger behind those words. He didn't blame her. Dent wasn't just power-hungry; he was a card-carrying dirtbag.

"We should keep this small," she added. "Just me and Agent Cyr. We'll apprehend him and bring him back."

The very thought of that had Thad's heart pumping in panic. "The hell you will! You two going in alone? That's a hard pass."

"Severance." The ice in Valenti's tone was clear warning that Thad had overstepped. He lifted a hand in apology, but there was nothing apologetic about the anger suffusing his veins. Elodie would go nowhere alone with that Akkadian if he had anything to say about it.

"I wouldn't have put it as bluntly as Captain Severance just did," Valenti said, "but I agree with the sentiment. I won't have my people going in without backup."

Dacina nodded as if she had expected as much. "Then we go in with a small task force. The chiral pilot and his counterpart. The chiral animal pairs."

"Chiral? Why?" Valenti asked sharply.

"His compound is like this room. Once we are inside, we will be unable to get a signal out."

"One big SCIF," Gabe murmured. "And the only thing it can't

block is the telepathic link all chiral pairs share."

"Indeed. Communication through quantum entanglement between the chiral pairs is unassailable."

"So that's why you need us," Valenti said. "Quantum telepathy."

"If that's so, then why was she willing to go in with just Ell?" Thad asked.

"The chiral pairs are not necessary, but they would be expedient," Dacina said with forced patience. "Especially since you refused my initial proposal to send in only myself and Agent Cyr."

Valenti considered that for a moment. "Very well. Tell us everything you know about Dent," she said.

"Dent's tastes are extravagant. He cultivates a reputation as a recluse, but the business he has set up for himself often requires that his company entertain. His compound has what you might call a public side. It includes villas, elaborate hanging gardens, exotic wildlife. The gardens require extensive maintenance."

"So we go in as gardeners," Micah said. "And Agent Cyr goes in as…"

"As part of the house staff."

"How do you know all this?" Valenti asked.

"From a contact inside Dent's compound."

Thad suspected that Akkadians cultivated their contacts differently from the way the Geminate Navy did things. Coercing innocents could backfire, too. The civilian being threatened could fabricate intel, thinking they were giving their tormenter what they wanted— especially if the truth was grim.

"Look, I have a buddy who did security on Venus after he left the Marines," Thad said. "I can reach out, see if he's in a position to help."

"Do it," Valenti ordered. With a decisive nod, she stood. "Mission approved. Severance, Case, Cyr—work with Dacina on a mission plan and get it to me ASAP. I'll be over at the NSA, filling in the director."

FOUR:
MISSION LAUNCH

GNS *WRAITH*
INBOUND FROM SOL'S CALABI-YAU GATE

This had to be one of the fastest mission workups Ell had ever done. She'd barely had time to turn her case work over to Quinn before she found herself kitted up and on board Micah's *Wraith*. Before local sunrise, the team was at the heliosphere, in the queue for gate transit between Procyon and Sol.

It had been decades since Ell had last visited the system that had birthed humanity. Thad and Micah had grabbed bunks aft and were sleeping. The animals were curled up in their crates in cargo, but they weren't confined—the doors were keyed to open at the slightest nudge of a paw.

Soft murmurs sounded from the cockpit, Jonathan conversing with his crew. Knowing sleep was going to elude her for some time, Ell unwebbed and moved forward.

"Can't sleep, huh?" Yuki asked when Ell neared her gunner's station.

"Nope." Ell stared out at the big tan-and-gold swirling gas giant they were approaching, captivated by its big red eye. "Figured I'd come up and sightsee for a bit."

"Ever been to one of the resorts on Ganymede? Man, it's been years," Nina, the crew chief, said wistfully.

Yuki snorted. "Yeah, that's been a rite of passage after Basic ever since I can remember. Right up there with blowing your first paycheck on a hotrod you'll never have time to drive—"

"—or wasting all your creds on virtual strippers," Jonathan finished, laughing.

"Dude, you did not. Seriously?" Katie, their co-pilot, turned to face him, her short-cropped blue hair the brightest spot of color in the cockpit. "I need all the deets. Leave nothing out. C'mon, spill!"

Jonathan eyed the gangly Sirian native like he would a puppy that hadn't been potty trained. Considering that Fred, Katie's mournful basset hound, was her constant companion and best friend, Ell thought that was an apt comparison.

"It's just a saying, Hyer. Like all dogs have fleas."

"Hey, Fred takes issue with that!"

"Fred's not here."

Before things degenerated any further, Ell insinuated herself into the conversation. "How long will it take to get to Venus from here?"

"We'll be docking at Jupiter's joint military base in about half an hour. From there, you, Thad, Micah, and the animals will move to a civilian vessel."

"I figured that much," she said dryly. "This is Coalition space. As far as they're concerned, we're a foreign military."

Jonathan grinned. "Yeah. Can't be flying around the Sol System in a Helios as if we own the place."

"Except you will be," Katie pointed out.

"Covertly. And only as backup in case you need a hot exfil. There's a difference."

Ell nodded. She wasn't a pilot so she didn't understand exactly how the direct action penetrator Jonathan flew could remain stealthy so deep in a star system like Sol, but she didn't doubt that it could. Katie's enthusiastic chatter about rootkit spyware and how they'd use it to access foreign systems went way above her head, and she'd never even heard of a BUSS drone.

"BUSS?" she asked.

"Oh yeah," Katie said. "Biomimetic Uncrewed Space Systems. They are *insane*."

Apparently, 'insane' meant that Jonathan could fool any security drone policing the area into thinking *Wraith* was a local ship. Or they could make the Sol drones ignore the Helios altogether.

Yuki jostled Jonathan's seat. "Hey, remind me again why Micah's going and not you? He's the chiral one. Shouldn't he be staying here with us where he won't get caught? You'd still have your woo-woo telepathic connection, doesn't matter which one of you goes."

Ell knew that one. "Dacina's contact says Dent's security uses biological agents."

Yuki's expression tightened. "That's illegal."

Dacina spoke up for the first time. "That does not make the threat any less real."

"Ya think?" Yuki snapped back.

Once more, Ell intervened. "It's because Micah's physiology makes him immune to biological agents. Same with Pascal and Sneaky Pete. If Dent's security has these and we can't circumvent them, the mission's still a go."

"Whoops! Hang tight, people. I'm getting pinged." Jonathan swung back around to face his holoscreen. He murmured something too low for Ell to catch, then called out, "Better go wake Thad and Micah. ETA to the base, fifteen mikes."

Transfer to the civilian bullet ship was uneventful, though Ell did experience a tense few moments: first, when Dacina, dressed in Marsian monastery garb, was asked to unveil her face, and second, when the bullet ship's SI tried to classify Pascal, the Ceriban hunting cat wearing the harness of a working animal, as an Earth predator known as a panther. She needn't have worried, though. Valenti's team had done an excellent job forging the big cat's papers, and whatever Akkadian trick Dacina used seemed to work equally well. In minutes, the group had passed through the scan and were in their seats. Shortly thereafter, the ship was on its way.

Finally, Ell was able to relax enough to catch some sleep. Not that it lasted long. In what felt like minutes, Thad was gently shaking her awake.

"We're here, *cher*. Want to check out the view?"

Ell suppressed a yawn and sat up, looking at the public holoscreen projected overhead. It showed the ship's forward sensor feed, a shot of Venus growing rapidly as they neared. Bright spots dotted around the planet's equator marked the location of the five major Lantern cities, so named for the massive chain of glowing ES fields that encompassed them.

A small ribbon of steel encircled the planet—one of the very few planetary rings in existence. There wasn't much of substance to the Venus Ring; unlike the science fiction stories that had made the concept so famous centuries ago, these rings weren't habitable. Instead, they were used as infrastructure, to help anchor the lantern cities, and to facilitate the transfer of goods and services between them in the same way a space elevator would on a planet whose surface pressure wasn't ninety-two times that of Earth.

The bullet ship docked at the Ring, and they disembarked. Thad led the way, following the signs that led them to baggage claim.

"Hold up," Katie said, stopping in the middle of the concourse. "Our bags aren't there. And neither are the animals' crates."

Thad steered her to one side and out of the traffic flow. "What do you mean?"

She shrugged. "I tagged them with a tracker. They're not where we're headed. They're that way." She pointed back the way they'd come.

"She is correct." Abruptly, Dacina turned and melted into the crowd.

"What the hell—?" Micah said.

He was interrupted by the assassin's mental voice. *{This way. They have been flagged and diverted to baggage holding.}*

Ell looked over at a glowering Thad. "She's efficient."

Thad cursed and headed back the way they'd come, following the map Dacina dropped onto their impromptu group comm channel. "I want to know how she did that," he said.

"Believe me, so do I," Ell said. *{Is there any explanation on why they were diverted?}* she asked Dacina.

{None.}

{So we hope for the best and prepare for the worst,} Micah said. *{Keep your balaclavas handy, folks.}*

Ell patted her ship suit vest to confirm that it was still there. The balaclavas were made of the same drakeskin metamaterial as their stealth suits. Drakeskin was standard issue for any spec op covert insertion, its transformation optics tunable to any environment. It gave the wearer a chameleon-like ability to blend into the background, or it could be programmed to look like whatever the wearer wished. Right now, their suits were configured to look like a basic ship's uniform.

When the baggage holding sign came into sight, Thad sped up until he was abreast of the assassin. *{Fall back and cover our six. I'll handle this,}* he said.

Dacina slowed to let Micah, Ell, and Katie pass. The area was surprisingly empty for a station of this size; when they arrived, there seemed to be no one staffing the counter.

Thad leaned over it and peered into the back. "Not a person in sight." He raised his voice. "Hello! Anyone home?"

The figure that stepped out of the shadows was a humanoid SI dressed in the livery of one of Sol's larger spacelines. "Can I help you, sir?" the synthetic intelligence asked.

Thad's smile turned fixed, which amused Ell. Apparently, his plan had been to charm the baggage handler. That wouldn't work so well on an SI.

He recovered quickly. "Yes. I understand you're holding our luggage. I need it back."

A projector emerged from the SI's torso. "Which flight, please. And names?"

Katie rattled off the information before Thad could respond.

{Get into position,} Ell said. *{If we're flagged as suspicious, we're only going to have a second to neutralize it before it brings security down on us.}*

FIVE:
BUM LEG

RING SPACEPORT
VENUS

Dacina nudged Thad aside and squared off with the SI. *{If it comes to that, I can take care of this one. The cameras in the hallway will need to be dealt with, though. There are three.}*

{How the hell did she find them so fast?} Katie asked Ell.

{She was studying the hallway while we were busy with the SI,} Ell replied.

She looked around. One camera was obvious, at the juncture between wall and ceiling. That left two more for them to find.

Katie drifted over to the 'substances not allowed' placard. *{Got one,}* she said. *{It's embedded in the top center of the frame.}*

{Here's the other one,} Micah said, bending down to examine a water dispenser.

With his height, Thad could take out the one in the ceiling just by driving his fist into the lens. *{Looks like this one's mine, cher. You get to cover all our asses. Or back up your assassin buddy. Your call.}*

"Ah, I see," the SI said, interrupting the mental tactics. "Yes, the belongings you declared do not show a paid customs duty fee. You owe two hundred seventy-three Sol credits for that, and another hundred each for the livestock you are bringing in. Your baggage will be secure here until payment is received. You may pay here." The image the SI projected changed, a transaction screen appearing beside the list of tagged baggage.

Ell nearly sagged in relief.

{Well, that's a letdown,} Micah said. *{And let's just agree now not to let Pascal know that he was labeled as livestock.}* Aloud, he added, "Thad, pay the nice SI and let's be on our way."

{Damn idiots,} Thad muttered, handing over a credit chit.

{Which idiots this time?} Ell asked.

{The people staffing the Geminate Navy garrison back at Jupiter. They should have taken care of the customs fee, or at least warned us about it.}

{Can't argue that. Thankfully, they got the Sol credits right when they loaded our credit chits. At least, the SI doesn't seem to be complaining about it,} she replied.

Once their bags had been ransomed and Pascal and Sneaky Pete retrieved, they headed back down the deserted hallway to the main concourse. Ell slung one of the duffels over her shoulder and took control of Pascal's maglev crate. Katie grabbed Pete's carrier and one of the long weapons cases disguised as luggage.

While Thad and Micah divvied up the remaining bags, Dacina looped her arms through a backpack that looked like it should have been heavier than she made it out to be. Her arms swung freely at her sides, though her hands remained close to the hidden pockets Ell knew from experience contained weapons of varying sizes.

They had gone no more than five meters, still well within the SI's sensor range, when the carbyne nerve fibers in Ell's leg gave out on her.

"Shit!" Shoving aside the pain drilling icepicks into her thigh, she tried desperately to catch herself with her one good leg. The awkward hop sent the duffel she carried banging hard against her side. Now hopelessly off balance, she fell.

Katie dropped the weapons bag and lunged to catch Ell, Sneaky Pete chittering in alarm. The bag broke open. Weapons, no longer concealed by the case's specialized Faraday shielding, spilled out onto the hallway floor.

Instantly, alarms blared, echoing throughout the corridor.

{*Camo!*} Thad yelled, pulling on his balaclava.

Ell did the same, activating her drakeskin suit as she rolled to her feet—both of which were now working again.

"Freeze!" the baggage SI called out. It cleared the counter in an agile move that only a security bot could make, and raced toward them, drawing a weapon that looked like the kind that would flash-bang/flash-blind.

{*Run!*} Micah yelled.

When Katie hesitated, Ell nudged her. {*Go! I'm good.*}

Katie, now nothing more than a transparent green outline on Ell's drakeskin head-up display, dove for one of the pistols and rolled into a full-on sprint, headed down the hall.

Micah mirrored her actions, grabbing Pascal's crate, which faded from view the moment he touched it.

Thad hooked a hand under Ell's arm. {*Need a lift?*}

Ell didn't bother with words, just raced to catch up to Micah, Katie, and the animals. {*Where's Dacina?*}

{*Last I saw, she was headed for that damned SI. She can take care of herself, cher.*}

{*Okay, so what's the plan?*}

{*Find or make a dead space where the station can't see us, then change identities. We've burned these. Good thing we all have spares. We can replace the weapons that we lost down on Illuminari.*}

Katie and Micah hooked a left down a cross corridor. Thad and Ell followed.

{*No joy! It's a dead end,*} Micah called out.

{*Wait! There's an office...*} Katie placed her palm against the door plate and applied a LockPik to hack it. It slid open and she pulled Pascal's crate in after her.

Micah had backtracked to the intersection. *{Don't think that's a good idea, Kate. We have a team of customs agents inbound!}*

{Gimme a minute! I've hacked the system, and I'm looking for a good hidey hole— Bingo! All right folks, follow me.}

{Not until you let me out of this crate,} Pascal growled.

{You can't be seen,} Ell objected.

{He's wearing the harness. If we activate it, he won't be seen,} Katie argued.

{In dark spaces! It's a simple cloaking device, not a friggin' drakeskin suit!} Thad yelled back.

{They will be too busy chasing me to be of concern,} Dacina's voice came calmly over the channel. *{Send me the rendezvous location. I will dispense with these and join you shortly.}*

{No killing, Dacina!} Ell called out.

There was a pause. *{Very well.}*

{You know, I think that's the Akkadian way of calling you a spoilsport, cher.} The green outline that was Thad opened Pascal's crate, and the big cat flowed out. *{Come on, Navy, let's get this done. Didn't know your young copilot was a hacker now. Where'd she pick that up? Not that I'm complaining.}*

{You can thank my twin's girlfriend for that one.}

Katie ignored the exchange, jogging past Ell to flank Micah's green outline on the other side of the intersection. *{This way.}*

There were several muffled thuds behind them, then silence.

{Sounds like the coast is clear,} Micah said, then, *{Aw, shit. Spoke too soon. Incoming! Team of six.}*

{Go high!} Thad ordered, as a second team of customs agents barreled around the corner.

Ell engaged her suit's organogel fibers and slapped her hand against the wall's smooth surface. It stuck. She pulled herself up, the millions of microscopic fibers lining the palms of her gloves, her suit's kneepads, and the soles of her boots giving her gecko-like capabilities.

A new icon showed up on her HUD, flashing first the red of a tango, then settling into green as her suit's system connected with Dacina's Akkadian camouflage. All around her, the team was scaling the walls—except for Dacina, and of course, Pascal.

She placed a hand on Pascal's flank, and they crouched, waiting for the oncoming agents to close on their position.

{Dacina,} Katie whispered.

Ell cut her off. {She knows what she's doing.}

A signal passed from Dacina to the hunting cat, who pressed himself against the far wall. Light glinted off a pair of throwing stars that the assassin sent flying, but they seemed to dissolve into nothing before they landed. This drew the attention of the oncoming guards, who shifted to one side just enough for Pascal to slip past.

"What the hell was that?" one guard asked.

"Hallway light flickering," the leader dismissed. "Come on."

Dacina vaulted effortlessly over the guard at the far end, who remained oblivious to her presence. When they disappeared around the bend, Ell lowered herself back to the floor.

{Let's go before they discover no one's down there,} Thad said. {Katie, you're on point.}

SIX:
ILLUMINARI

ILLUMINARI RING ELEVATOR
VENUS SPACEPORT

The 'black hole' Katie had found—a storage closet—was so cliché that Micah joked about it the entire time they switched their biosigs over to fresh cover identities. Once they'd made the swap, Thad released a surveillance microdrone into the hallway. When a lull came in foot traffic, they slipped out in staggered waves, merging unobtrusively with the crowd.

It occurred to Ell that Sneaky Pete was being unusually quiet, and she wondered if their encounter with the customs agents had traumatized the ferret. She fell back so that she was walking alongside Katie and peered down into the carrier slung over her shoulder.

And got a face full of something that smelled… like pine? She jerked her head back fast, wiping the spray from her eyes as Sneaky Pete's *{oops}* sounded inside her head.

Thad grabbed her elbow as she stumbled blindly into him.

"You okay, *cher*?" he asked.

"Pete found something—" she wheezed, "—got me with it—"

It was hopeless, the fragrance too strong. Ell broke into a fit of coughing.

"Sneaky Pete!" Katie scolded. "You do *not* spray people in the face. That's just rude!"

"What *was* that thing?" Ell rasped, her eyes still stinging, though her military medical nano was quickly clearing the sensation.

{Was shiny! Didn't know smelly, too.} The ferret sounded disappointed.

"Give me that," Katie demanded, shoving her hand inside the carrier. The disk she pulled from Pete's grip was indeed shiny. "It's one of those bathroom scent thingies, I think," she said, examining it closely. "He must have swiped it from the closet when I wasn't looking."

{Was shiny,} the ferret repeated. His sulky tone implied they never let him have *any* fun. It was the exact same tone Snotface would have taken, yet another indicator that the chiral ferret was identical to him in every way.

Pascal, wearing a harness that proclaimed him to be a working cat, dragged Micah over to Katie so that he could inspect the thing in her hand. The big cat took one big sniff and his lips pulled back, exposing his fangs. *{Stupid ferret. It's not even edible.}*

To Pascal's misfortune, the carrier was still open. Worse, Sneaky Pete had great aim. A second disk, which Katie had missed, scored a hit right on Pascal's nosepad, wringing a yelp from him.

{Am not stupid! Not!}

"Whoa there, tiger," Micah said, pulling Pascal away. Ell wasn't quite sure who that comment was meant for.

"We know you're not," Katie said soothingly, giving Sneaky Pete a quick pat on the head, then sealing the carrier. "You're very smart for a ferret."

"Three-ring circus," Thad said to himself, though it was pitched loud enough for everyone to hear. His eyes rose to the ceiling as if in prayer. "I don't have a team, I have a flippin' three-ring circus."

That caused everyone but Dacina to laugh. The whole encounter lightened the collective mood—and that was a good thing for OPSEC, as far as Ell was concerned. One of the first rules of operational security was to blend in. In her opinion, a small knot of people walking tensely through a concourse fell far short of that.

Everyone remained quiet during the short walk to the tram that would take them down to Illuminari. Ell figured they'd had enough excitement for one day; she just hoped that fate saw things that way, too, and would cut them a break.

{So far, so good,} Micah said. But there was unease in his voice, and he kept glancing around.

Ell understood the feeling. She still half-expected guards to rush them from out of nowhere, exposing them as undercover Geminate agents, here illegally.

{Do your people not have a saying?} Dacina asked. *{'No battle survives first contact with the enemy'? This is to be expected.}*

{Yeah. Sun Tzu,} Micah said. *{But you knew that, right? He was your ancestor, not mine.}*

{Akkadia was settled mostly from the ancient middle east, not Asia,} she replied, then looked away as if the conversation had lost interest for her.

Ell gave Micah a wordless shrug. She, too, had the sense that he'd somehow offended Dacina, even if mildly, but she had no idea why.

They moved again as the queue for the tram shifted. While they were waiting, Ell asked Thad, "What's your friend like? What was his name? Ken?"

"Yeah. You know the type. Enlists, gets his first month's pay, does exactly what the drill instructor says not to do. Real hard case, but steady as they come."

"Okay, so which thing did he do?" Katie asked. "Buy a hot aircar for zero down at a crazy interest rate… or marry a stripper?"

"He married a stripper."

Ell laughed. "You're kidding."

"Nope."

"Right. Next thing you're going to tell us is her name is Bambi," Micah joked.

"Actually…"

Thad drew the word out so long it made Ell laugh. "You guys have it all wrong. It's *Barbie* and Ken, not Bambi."

"No, it's not. It's Bambi. You know, like the cabbage patch kids, Bambi and Ken."

Katie guffawed. "Dude, you have your old Earth history *allll* screwed up. And you," she poked Thad in the shoulder, "are pulling our legs."

"Swear to God, *petit-soeur*. Her name is Bambi."

Dacina remained impassive, but the look in her eyes told Ell that their banter was an entirely new experience for her.

Good, she thought. *That'll give her something else to benchmark against her own culture.*

They were getting close enough that Ell could see the trams that took passengers down. It looked like the maximum number of people per tram was ten. She counted heads. Their group of five would have to share—unless Pascal's presence scared off the locals. She made a mental bet with herself that it would.

She was right. The people behind them hesitated just long enough for the SI monitoring the trams to beep a warning, and then the doors slid shut, sealing them all in. Thad made himself comfortable, then scowled when Pascal jumped up on the bench beside him and sprawled half on his lap.

"Mangy mutt, get your own bench."

{They're all taken. Besides, the plas is cold on my paws. Your lap is warmer.}

Micah, seated on the bench across from him, grinned. "Aww look at that. You're a kitty paw warmer."

"Shut it, Navy." Thad gave the pilot what was apparently supposed to be his fiercest glower. But because there was no real threat, it just came off as 'get-off-my-lawn' grumpy. Then he turned it on the cat. "You want to use my lap as a paw warmer? Fine. But it'll cost you. Three steaks."

Ell couldn't quite suppress the laugh that threatened to escape. The ongoing feud between Pascal and Thad was legendary. Last she'd heard, the big cat had extorted somewhere north of a hundred and fifty steaks out of him.

Thad switched his glare to Ell. "I'm wounded, *cher*."

"Sorry."

She turned her head away to hide her grin, and her gaze was snagged by the spectacle of light below. The lantern city was approaching fast, its ES shield sparkling an iridescent blue. But it was the display inside the field that captured her attention. It seemed that every building and every street was painted with light; the soft, golden outlines gave it a fairy-like appeal.

"It's beautiful," Katie said.

"Yes, it is."

"Do not be taken in by appearances." Dacina said as they stood to disembark. Her warning was one of the rare times she had chosen to speak on the way here. "You will soon see. The Gaming District here is different. And very dangerous."

SEVEN:
GAMING DISTRICT

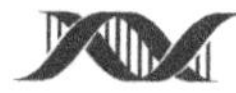

Lower Levels
Lantern City of Illuminari
Venus

Three hours later, and several tiers below the ring's main level, Ell had to admit Dacina was right.

She accessed the private team channel. *{As many years as I've served in special forces, you'd think I would have seen it all. But wow.}*

{This'll stretch your definition of excess, for sure,} Micah agreed.

{Funny how it's always the lower levels, isn't it?} Thad said.

That got a mental grunt out of Dacina.

Truthfully, mental conversations were about the only way they could communicate in Illuminari's Gaming District. Ell could feel the deep bass of music in her bones, layered beneath the electronic clamor of gambling. The sounds engulfed them, seeming to come from everywhere all at once.

Adding to the sensory overload were lights that strobed, cutting through air hazy with substances that the sensors in her drakeskin suit identified as not entirely legal.

The crowd alternated between pressing their group uncomfortably close and ripping them asunder. Thad's imposing physique was the spear of the wedge, Micah and Dacina each operating as wings. Katie and Ell were tucked in behind, with Pascal pacing between them and the blue-haired pilot holding the strap to Sneaky Pete's carrier in an iron grip.

Dacina's face was blank, as usual. In contrast, Katie's was a blend of fascination and incredulity. Her eyes bounced everywhere, trying to take in everything all at once.

Holosigns carried by microdrones floated all around, declaring 'Live Dancers!' and 'Feats That Defy the Imagination!' The busker in front of the entrance to the comedy house—human or SI, Ell couldn't tell which—called out in piercing tones, waving people in to see tonight's act.

Katie leaned in close so Micah could hear and shouted over the din. "Hey Cap, you bring me to the nicest places!"

Micah grinned but didn't respond.

And then they were through the worst of it, beyond the ring of cacophony that first assaulted those traveling down from above.

{Something tells me the people who own and run this level aren't subjected to this madhouse,} Micah mused.

{They are not. But we cannot afford the same luxury. To bypass it would draw unwanted attention. This, I think we can agree, is not in our best interest,} Dacina said. That was a lot, coming from the Dagger. *{We turn here,}* she added abruptly, fitting action to her words.

Thad matched her fast turn, Micah keeping pace beside him. Ell hooked a hand through Katie's elbow, steering her away from a collision with an oncoming oil-slicked performer dressed in leather, feathers, and very little else.

{Your tongue's hanging out,} Ell teased as Katie's head whipped around to follow the guy.

*{The old man would ground me for **weeks** if he knew I was here,}* Katie said, half in jest. *{Sneaky Pete, cover your eyes.}*

Dacina stopped in front of a door and input a code, then gave Ell a pointed look that said the assassin had little patience for the color commentary coming from her companions. The door opened and she ducked inside. Ell and the rest followed.

No more words were exchanged until they made it down to the hotel room the assassin had acquired, and even then, none were spoken aloud until a thorough sweep had been made and surveillance countermeasures put in place.

"Have you heard from your contact, Dacina?" Ell asked.

"No. But I did not expect to. I left a signal on our way here and retrieved Dent's address at the drop point. She will find the signal and we will meet later tonight."

"Wow, you're good. I never saw you leave a signal or retrieve anything," Katie said, looking up from where she was examining the small food printer in the kitchenette.

Micah laughed. "That's because you were too busy rubbernecking."

Katie jammed her hands on her hips and gave him a challenging look. "And you did?"

When Micah didn't respond, she smirked. "That's what I thought." She returned her attention to Dacina. "Any chance your friend could hook us up with some formation blocks so we can use this thing? It'd be sweet if she could swing a couple of bricks of ActiveFiber, too."

Dacina didn't answer immediately, fixing dark eyes on Katie. Such scrutiny would have made an average person uneasy; Katie gave no indication it affected her in the slightest.

"I have read in your file about your skill with the Fiber," Dacina said at length. "You are… inventive."

"You can say that again," Micah said under his breath. He and Thad had taken a seat on the sofa. On the low table in front of them were spread all the disassembled weapons parts they had smuggled in, save for the one case they'd spilled at customs.

"Uh, is that a yes?" Katie asked Dacina.

"Yes. I will procure this for you." The assassin turned away— more like *glided* away, Ell thought—to conduct a more thorough inspection of the room.

{*And steaks,*} Pascal said from where he lay under the coffee table. {*Need steaks.*}

"You will be fed, cat," Dacina said,

Ell moved over to where Thad and Micah sat. "Well, I guess that's that," she said in an undertone.

Thad spared a hard look down at the slumbering cat. "How come he listens to her and never to me?"

One green eye opened. {*Heard that.*}

Ell smiled. "How's it looking?" she asked Micah.

He pointed to the holoscreen. "We have surveillance bots posted here, here, and here." He tagged spots on the hallway outside their room and at the lifts that led upward. "So far, everything's quiet."

"Good." She nudged Thad. "When do you meet with Ken?"

"He just responded. He gets off work in about an hour. He'll go home, change, then ping me directions to a local watering hole. I'll meet him there. "

"Good," Dacina said, turning away from her inspection. "This gives us opportunity. Come." She took a seat at the kitchenette's tiny table and pulled out a bundle of long, needle-like bamboo sticks.

Katie stepped away from the food printer to get a closer look. "What are those?"

"Tebori." Dacina moved another chair so that it faced her, and waved Ell toward it. "Sit. This takes time. We begin now."

The needles looked sharp. Ell wondered what kind of Akkadian ritual Dacina was proposing. "Begin what?" she asked.

"Giving you the mark of *zhídé de duìshǒu.*"

EIGHT:
MARKED

HOTEL ROOM
ILLUMINARI, VENUS

Ell stared at Dacina in disbelief. Was she serious? Here they were, deep in the heart of the Sol system, without authorization, in the middle of an op, and Dacina wanted to do— what? She didn't even know what tebori was. The Akkadian equivalent of doing each other's nails?

"Uh no, if it's all the same, I'll pass, thanks."

The Dagger's hand whipped out impossibly fast, tagging her at the juncture between her natural and cloned leg. "Here."

"What? No!"

"Why?" Micah's voice was close, and it sounded… different, like he'd caught onto a subtext that had somehow eluded Ell.

"Tebori commemorates many things. For the Tèzhŏng, it is often used to honor scars received in battle."

Ell took a step back. "Oh no, I'm good, thanks. I don't need to commemorate an incident, which, by the way, I never told you about. I don't know what you've read in the file Akkadia has on me, but believe me when I tell you, I'm reminded of that battle—every single day."

"Indeed. But this is not why I offer. There is another, more important reason." Dacina's dark eyes grew intense, almost hypnotic. "No one, other than the Tèzhŏng, has ever been given such. As the bearer of this symbol, you will be able to go anywhere on Akkadia without fear of being challenged."

"Whoa…" Katie sounded intrigued. "She'd be, like, the first ever Geminate Navy Akkadian assassin. That is so seriously cool."

"No." Dacina looked amused. "She is not beaded."

"And I'm fine with that, by the way," Ell said.

"Just my two creds," Micah said, "but this sounds like a rare opportunity. Why not? What other plans do we have for tonight?"

Micah's response surprised Ell. More, it made her step back and think objectively about the offer, rather than going with her first knee-jerk reaction. She looked over to see what Thad thought.

He shrugged. "Sounds like maybe the Akkadian version of an honorary degree. It's up to you, *cher.*" He turned to Dacina. "Anything special about the ink you use? Or the needles? Not that I don't trust you, but the last thing Ell needs is for you to be inserting some tracking nano under her skin under the pretense of giving her some Sisterhood tat."

"There are many tattoo kiosks near here," Dacina said patiently. "The Venusian government has strict regulations on the materials used in body alteration. You supply the dyes, I will use the traditional reeds. You may scan them first, but I assure you, they are safe."

Ell couldn't believe she was actually considering doing this. But Micah was right; this was a once-in-a-lifetime opportunity. And she could always have it removed back home if she didn't like it. She blew out a breath. "Okay. Where do we start?"

Dacina pointed to Micah. "You buy the inks. I will accompany you. We return before Captain Severance leaves to meet his contact."

They were back sooner than Ell had anticipated. When she

remarked on it, Micah shrugged. "There was a kiosk literally across the street."

"Any suspicious activity?" Thad asked.

"None that we saw."

A quick look at Dacina told Ell that the assassin agreed with Micah's assessment.

"Come. We begin." Dacina retrieved her needles from Katie and moved to the table.

Ell hesitated, still not convinced this was the best use of their time.

"Go ahead," Thad said. "We can't do anything but look through the local net until I hear back from Ken or Dacina heads out to her meetup."

She was out of excuses, so she gave in and sat down. Thad pulled up a chair to watch.

The bamboo reeds were laid out on an oiled cloth that didn't look terribly sanitary. She was relieved when Dacina pulled out a sterilization unit and motioned for her to bare her leg. Ell used blink commands to create a seam down the leg of the drakeskin suit; she peeled it back and Dacina ran the sterilizer over the skin just above the knee.

"Isn't this an odd place for a tattoo?" she asked when Dacina reached for the first needle.

"There are no odd places for art."

Well, I guess that's that, then, Ell thought sardonically. She bit her lip and managed, just barely, not to jerk when the reed first bit into her thigh.

Thad, on the other hand, looked like *he* was the one who had been jabbed. He jumped to his feet. "Got to go, Ken just pinged."

The rapid rate at which he left the hotel room was comical. "Some guys just don't like needles, I guess," she murmured.

Ell soon realized that though the process was painful, it wasn't anything she couldn't handle. Dacina's head was bent while she worked, giving Ell the chance to study the Akkadian more closely without being caught staring. The assassin had several tattoos of her own—the most prominent one marched up her outer arm to her shoulder.

All in black, it looked like a stylized peacock feather that ended with a hilt and handle where the quill would ordinarily be. The fanciful blade was beautiful.

Another tattoo twined around her ankle like a snake, and might actually be a snake, but from where Ell sat, it disappeared up Dacina's pant leg. With the reeds moving so rapidly in and out of her own thigh, Ell didn't think it wise to bend down and inspect it.

It occurred to her that she'd agreed to this without even knowing what the final design would look like. When she asked, Dacina's response was vague. "The needles know," was all she would say.

Ell felt a small flare of annoyance at that. Maybe it was cultural, maybe not. Either way, Dacina was taking this mystical stuff a little far.

When she was done, though, Ell couldn't argue with the results. The design wound around her leg like a band; long, curving strokes formed a chain that felt curiously organic. Layered on top were a series of intricate swirls, made from what seemed like a million tiny dots. It was as exotic as it was beautiful.

"Use the med kit to dose yourself with a painkiller," the assassin instructed as she cleaned her reeds and returned them to one of the many sheaths strapped to her body.

"I would have thought that part of the ritual was toughing out the recovery without anesthetic," Ell said, staring down at her lower thigh.

"Where is the practicality in that? We move on Dent's estate tomorrow. You will not wish to be impaired."

Ell flexed her leg. It was tender, but surprisingly free of neuropathic pain.

Dacina headed for the door. "I leave now. I will be back before Captain Severance returns." Without another word, she was gone.

NINE:
OLD FRIENDS

VORTEX & VAPOR CASINO BAR
ILLUMINATI GAMING DISTRICT

Thad had no trouble locating the bar Ken had named for their meetup. The place was off the main strip, which meant drink prices were still high, but not exorbitant. The SI at the entrance screened him when he arrived, but remained silent—testament to the excellent cover the SRU had provided.

He spotted Ken immediately, unsurprised to find him seated at the bar ringing the dance floor. With a resigned sigh, he wove his way through the crowd over to the former Marine. It seemed some things never changed.

Ken looked up at his approach, recognition in his eyes—and something else too fleeting for Thad to get a good read on. Resentment, possibly. If so, that was just too bad. Thad wasn't responsible for the choices Ken had made, or the path where they had led.

Ken rose to greet him, hooking a hand around Thad's and pulling him close in a back-thumping hug. "How ya been, brother?

Good to see you. What brings you all the way out here?" He gestured for Thad to take a seat beside him.

Thad briefly thought about suggesting an alternate meeting place, one where strippers wouldn't be bending their bodies close enough for credits to be shoved into impossibly skimpy scraps of fabric, then thought better of it. Sometimes, this kind of place provided the best cover. It would take some seriously high-end surveillance equipment to filter their conversation out of the heavy bass beat and the raised voices of the crowd that, despite the early hour, was substantial.

Besides, if that didn't work… With a single thought, Thad released a small cloud of audio chaff—microscopic attenuators bonded to lighter-than-air colloids.

Ken noticed immediately. "That's some serious shit, bro. I didn't know chaff was available outside Navy combat suits."

"And you still don't know that," Thad said, flashing his friend an easy smile. "Does Bambi know you're here?"

Ken shrugged, the smile falling from his face. "No reason for her to. We split six months ago."

That surprised Thad. Ken had been crazy about Bambi, and she about him; he'd always thought their marriage was one of the good ones, destined to last. "Hey, sorry man."

Ken waved away Thad's sympathy, surprisingly indifferent to the loss. "Old news. What can I do for you? Or should I say, what can I do for the Navy?"

Thad shook his head. "Not working for them any longer, hoss." It was true, in its own way. Task Force Blue, which he now led, was run by the NSA, not the Navy, though he and the rest of the team still held their commission and their ranks.

Ken's brow rose in surprise. "Thaddeus Severance the Third, no longer with the Geminate Navy? Dude, I had you pegged as a lifer."

"Can you help me or not?"

The former Marine lifted his hands. "Your story to tell, I respect that. Sure, I'm always happy to help a brother out. What exactly do you need?"

Thad laid a business card-sized plas sheet down on the bar between them and tapped it. Ken knew the routine; he picked it up, Thad's touch granting him access to the information it contained.

Ken gave a low whistle. "What do you plan to do, rob a bank?"

"No, nothing like that. Just doing a little cleanup for a friend. Can you fill the order? You'll be compensated."

Ken stared down at the card. "Yeah, sure. When do you need it?"

"I can follow you back to your place now." Under the cover of taking back his card, Thad slipped the former Marine a credit chit. "As you can see, money's no problem."

Ken's expression went blank, but he was thinking hard about it—Thad could see it in his eyes. The credit chit went into his pocket as he stood. He flagged down the SI servebot, tossed back his drink, and closed out his tab. "Right, then. Follow me."

Ken led Thad to a warehouse that sat in a transition zone between an office park and low income row houses. This time of day, the area was largely empty of curious eyes. Small children tossed a ball into a metal hoop driven into the dirt at the edge of a barren playground.

"Here we go." Ken unlocked the door and slid it back far enough for Thad to enter. The fact that the rust-flecked door didn't screech as it moved along equally rusted rails told Thad that it was well-maintained, despite its ramshackle appearance.

Ken spoke a word and light flared, illuminating rows of pallets stacked neatly, five high. He rolled the door shut and locked it, then headed down the nearest aisle. "I've got what you're looking for down here someplace."

Thad wasn't sure that what he was seeing was entirely legal, but that didn't concern him right then. He'd say whatever needed saying to complete his mission, and he knew Ken would be expecting a reaction out of him.

He whistled, long and low, as if impressed by what he saw.

"Brother, if contract work pays well enough for you to finance all this, then I'm in the wrong line of work."

"I could always use someone as skilled and dependable as you. My client list has grown recently, and I'm always on the lookout for good muscle."

Thad laughed. "Muscle, huh? What do I look like to you, hoss? A thug?"

Ken reappeared with a case of ammo in one hand, spare power packs in the other. "What do you think I do for a living? This is legitimate security work. Take a look around you. You know as well as I do that gaming districts can attract trouble. The people who own big business around here pay very well to keep visitors safe."

"You have a point. Tell you what, I'll think about it and let you know." Thad took the cases, then lifted them in a small salute of thanks.

He turned to leave, and then it occurred to him that Ken might have done work for Asher Dent under whatever alias he was using to do business here on Venus. Thad didn't know the name Dent was using, but he did have the address that Dacina's Akkadian contact had provided.

It would be a risk to ask Ken if he knew anything about the compound, but Thad judged it to be a minor one. He trusted a former Marine a hell of a lot more than he did a foreign assassin he'd yet to meet.

"One more thing…" Thad pulled out the small plas rectangle again and pushed the address to it. "Have you ever done any work at this location?"

The look Ken gave him was calculating. "Brother you play for high stakes, don't you? No, I can't say that I have, but I know of the place."

"Anything you can tell me about it?"

Ken flipped the plas card to a blank screen and began sketching with his fingertip in the air above it. A rough drawing emerged. "Now, this is all hearsay, you understand. I was in the compound once before, but under the old management, so I can't vouch for what changes might have been done since then."

He worked for a bit, paused to give it a last once-over, then handed it back to Thad. "Best I can do for you, brother. That, and a warning. If that's your mission, then wave off. The guy's friendly enough, but he's not one you want to mess with, you hear me?"

"Five by," Thad said. "Thanks."

"Don't thank me. Here's where we part ways, old friend." Ken unlocked the door and moved aside so that Thad could step through.

Thad looked back at Ken. "I owe you one, brother."

Ken's laugh was short. "You have no idea."

* * *

Ken watched the dark, solidly built man disappear in the distance. There was no mistaking the soldier; despite what he'd claimed about leaving the Navy, Ken didn't believe him for one second.

Once Thad's form was swallowed up by the night, Ken blinked a command and his implant made a call. When the person on the other end answered, his message was brief.

{He's here, and if the amount of ammo he requested is any indication, he's not alone.} He paused to listen to the words spoken on the other end. *{No worries. We'll be ready.}*

TEN:
COVERS

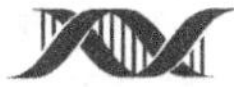

SAFE HOUSE
GAMING DISTRICT

Thad beat Dacina back by a matter of minutes. Ell unloaded one of the cases while Thad handled the other one, adding to the existing collection of weapons on the coffee table.

"Did he want to know why you needed these?" she asked.

"Nope, but he's a smart guy. He knows something's up. I did get some info on Dent's compound, though. He did security work there for the previous owner." Thad handed Katie the plas card and she scanned it into the portable unit she was using to search Illuminari's public net.

"Was that the best thing to do? Can he be trusted?" Micah asked.

"He was steady and reliable in the Marines. And there's not much he can do with the info I gave him—it's just an address."

"But he also knows about the power packs and ammo you bought from him," Ell pointed out. "Wouldn't be hard to put two and two together."

"That goes the other way, too. He knows by supplying me, it could implicate him. I'm betting he'll stay quiet. Besides, considering our intel's coming from an Akkadian, getting third party corroboration is never a bad idea."

"If that third party can be trusted," she said. "Don't forget, the Akkadians are as motivated as we are to take him down—maybe more. Their reputation was bad enough before Dent came into power. Then he's made Premier, commits acts of war against every star nation in the Coalition, then disappears, leaving Akkadia holding the bill, so to speak."

"You're really saying you trust an Akkadian over a former Marine," Thad said flatly.

"No one wants to find him and make him pay more than they do. I believe that."

"You question our motives, Captain?" Dacina had entered the room so quietly, no one had heard.

"How did you get by the security drones?" Micah asked.

"I programmed them to ignore me."

The Akkadian sheathed her blades and tossed a data chit onto the coffee table.

"Your covers. Memorize them."

Katie transferred the chit's contents over to her comp unit. "Got 'em." She turned on the unit's holoprojector.

"I'm going in with catering?" Ell asked.

"Dent is hosting an event in his gardens tomorrow night. There will be a sizable crowd. It will be our best opportunity to take him."

Ell kept reading. "Thad, you and Micah are working security. You're listed as an animal handler for a working cat."

Pascal padded over from the corner where he'd been napping. He rose onto his hind legs and settled his front paws on the sofa back with a hard thump. {Good. Parties have food. Many steaks.}

Katie gave him a stern look. "You'll be working, Pascal. Food is for the guests."

Pascal yawned wide, sharp incisors flashing in the overhead

lights. *{They won't miss one or two.}*

"Yeah, right. Just don't blow it for us." Katie returned her attention to the holo. "Hey, where's my cover?"

"You will remain here and provide intel for the team. My contact has placed several remote sensing devices around the property's perimeter. You will monitor," Dacina said.

That didn't sit well with Katie.

"You're the pilot, we're the door kickers, remember?" Thad said. "It's what we're trained to do."

"Micah's a pilot."

"Yeah, well, he's seen more action than you."

Ell winced. Thad's response wasn't just lame; he was clearly hedging. If there was one thing Katie Hyer hated with a passion, it was someone trying to 'handle' her. Ell waited for the dressing-down she was sure would come.

Katie settled back into the sofa and gave Thad a look that said he was full of shit and she was having none of it. "I do seem to recall combat training during my runup with Task Force Blue," she drawled.

Gone was the exuberant, wide-eyed young woman who had gawked at everything in sight on their way here. Ell realized she'd been lulled into seeing the side of Katie she wanted people to see, instead of the skilled and wickedly smart special forces pilot she was.

Thad realized his mistake and tried to backpedal. "Look, *petit-soeur*, if we're made, that blue hair of yours is going to be advertising your position like a big ol' target."

She sat up abruptly and, with the snap of her fingers, changed her hair to an unremarkable brown. "Any other objections? Or did you forget I swapped out the dye in my hair for carbon nanotubes, *for this very freakin' reason!* And don't you *petit-soeur* me, Thaddeus Severance. I am *not* your baby sister, and I do not need protecting any more than Ell or Micah or…or… Dacina."

Micah chuckled. "You stepped in it this time, Thad."

Thad glowered at him. "Shut up, Navy." He dropped his head

and went silent for a moment. If Ell knew him, it was half to rein in his temper and half to give himself time to genuinely consider what Katie had said. After a moment, he looked back up. "You're right. And sometimes that blue hair of yours makes me forget you're not my kid sister. Sorry, *cher*." He paused. "But that does not negate the fact that we need someone to remain here as overwatch. Dacina's plan is a good one. Much as I hate to admit it, pairing me and Pascal is the right call. That gives two of our three people access to Jonathan and the ship via the chiral pairs in case Dent's security for the night calls for frequency jammers."

Ell looked more closely at the roster and realized Thad was right. Just as Micah and Jonathan shared an unbreakable mental connection, so did Pascal with Joule, his chiral clone. It was the same with Snotface and Sneaky Pete.

Micah's grin bordered on wicked. "Jonathan's going to *love* playing switchboard operator for the ferrets and the cats."

"All right, I see your point," Katie said. "But I reserve the right to back you up if things go to hell."

"If that should occur, you may need this." Dacina handed her a formation brick.

"ActiveFiber! Thanks for remembering." Katie turned it over in her hands. "Oh yeah, I can do a lot with this…" She blanked the holo and got to work fiddling with the material.

ActiveFiber could be molded into just about any form imaginable—and Ell knew just how imaginative Katie was; she'd heard the stories. In Katie's hands, that unimposing gray block could become a very different kind of lethal weapon—the kind people tended to either overlook or dismiss.

"One more thing," Thad said. "We're going to need a solid exfil plan."

"Indeed. My contact informs me that Dent's estate has a small hangar bay belowground. It is built into the steel plating that forms the lantern city's base, and it opens out into the atmosphere of Venus," Dacina told them.

The pieces all fit together now. "Of course he'd have a fast getaway," Ell said. "Isn't that his M.O.?"

"In this case, it works in our favor," Micah pointed out. "Once we get inside, we don't have to fight our way back out. We can coordinate with Jonathan, and he sends us one of *Wraith*'s drones to cover us as we fly Dent's escape ship away from Illuminari."

They spent some time poking holes in the plan and factoring in contingencies, then the discussion wound down.

Katie and Micah resumed monitoring the feeds, and Thad turned his attention back to the weapons.

From somewhere on her person, Dacina produced a soft woven mat, removed her shoes and her cloak, and positioned her body in a way that looked familiar. Then she moved, flowing effortlessly from one defensive or offensive position to the next. The kata looked both graceful and deadly… and was fascinating to observe.

With Micah and Katie and Thad all occupied, that left Ell at loose ends. She sank into the overstuffed chair and watched Dacina's lethal dance. What seemed like moments later, Thad was gently shaking her shoulder; she had dozed off.

"Why don't you get some shuteye, *cher?* I'll take first watch."

With a yawn, she stood. "Good idea. Wake me and I'll take the next one."

ELEVEN:
RECON

Gaming District

When she awoke the next morning, it was to softly spoken conversation in the other room, and something rich and aromatic coming from the kitchenette. She sat up. Micah was sleeping on top of the second bed. Since he'd relieved her when third watch began, he must have only recently sacked out. She stepped quietly so as to not disturb the sleeping pilot.

Katie looked like she hadn't moved from the sofa. Her unit was on, the holoscreen's light playing across her features and her still-brown hair.

"Find anything?" Ell asked.

"Yep. I've been researching his alias." She input something into the unit and the screen flickered. "Dane Ashcroft of Shade Lock Industries, you have been a busy man," she said, more to herself than anyone else.

"Anything we can use to hang him with?" Thad asked, coming to stand beside Ell.

"No. Everything I can find indicates his business is a legit, legal entity—at least by Illuminari state code," Kate said with a tired sigh. She scrubbed her face vigorously with her hands, then unwound her crossed legs and stood. When she stretched her back, it popped.

"You know, if Sam heard that, she'd be sealing you inside a med unit for a scan, *cher*."

Katie swung her arms from side to side, loosening her upper torso. "Hazard of the job." She stopped and sniffed, as if just now noticing the aroma of coffee drifting in from the kitchenette. "Ooh, caffeine…"

She trailed Ell over to where Dacina stood working the food printer. Whatever concoction she was brewing, it smelled delicious.

Katie grabbed two cups and handed Ell one. "Got extra?" she asked the assassin.

Dacina filled Katie's cup. Katie took an appreciative sniff, then sampled it. If her response was any indication, it tasted incredibly bitter.

"What *is* this?" she sputtered.

Ell accepted her own cup from Dacina and took a sip. As expected, it was rich and bold, but held a bitterness that wasn't present in the drink she'd been served on Akkadia. "It's coffee—I think."

"It would be inaccurate to call it coffee," Dacina said. "But it is the best this machine can reproduce, so you may call it that."

Katie scooched between Dacina and the food printer. "No offense, but this isn't like any coffee I've ever tasted. This stuff would melt a spoon."

Ell could have sworn there was amusement in Dacina's eyes as Katie dialed in a heaping dose of cream, sweetener, and something else Ell didn't catch. The assassin stepped away to give Katie more room.

"What the Geminate call coffee is not," she said with a challenge-at-your-peril finality.

"Uh huh," was all Katie would say.

"What's the plan, Dacina?" Ell asked. "Recon?"

"Yes. As soon as your chiral pilot is awake, we go."

They split up, Ell and Thad going first, followed by Katie and Micah. Dacina, as usual, went her own way. The gaming district's lower level was busy, which made it easy to blend in. Part of their special forces training was in mimicking one's environment and looking unremarkable. Forgettable. But Dacina elevated that to another level entirely. Between one blink and the next , she was gone.

"She had to be using some sort of tech embedded in her street clothes," Thad said, searching in vain for the assassin.

"They do. Quinn once told me that."

"*Cher*, I'm beginning to worry about that assistant of yours," Thad said. "He's way too interested in assassins, if you ask me—" His words were truncated by an *ooph* as he bumped into someone moving hurriedly in the other direction. "Excuse me, ma'am…"

The woman he'd bumped into looked up at him in surprise. "Thad? Omigod, Thad Severance! What are you doing here?"

Only someone who knew Thad well could see his frustration. Being identified by *anyone*, friend or foe, while on an op was never a good thing.

Thad bypassed the question and instead said, "I saw Ken last night. I didn't know about you two. I'm sorry."

Bambi's eyes welled up and she gripped his forearm. "He changed, Thad." She wiped her tears away furiously with her free hand. "We never should have left the Procyon system and come to Sol."

Ell stepped closer, but wasn't sure exactly how to mitigate the nascent drama.

Thad patted Bambi's hand awkwardly. "I'm sorry, *cher*. You two seemed to fit. Thought you'd be in it for the long haul."

"He was fine until he started working security for all those rich guys. Greed, Thad. Don't ever let it rule you." She touched the pendant hanging from a silver chain around her neck. Lifting it so that it sat on her palm, she said, "I still have your gift. It reminds me of happier times."

With the press of her thumb, the pendant activated, and a small holo of two smiling people, obviously in love, stared out at Ell. One was Bambi. The other had to be Thad's Marine buddy, Ken.

"I'm so sorry," Ell said. "Maybe a trip home to Ceriba would help? Being around family and friends?"

Bambi looked aghast, her blonde curls bouncing as she shook her head vehemently. "But then I wouldn't be here if Ken changed his mind."

Ell exchanged a look with Thad, silently telling him they needed to leave, now. With a slight nod, Thad wrapped Bambi's fingers around the locket, the action disconnecting the holo.

"How about you give me your comm ID and we'll talk about this later? Think about what my good friend here just said. If you need a ride back home, I can help. Afraid I can't talk right now, we're on our way to meet someone."

Bambi sniffled in that helpless way some women affected to elicit sympathy from unwitting men.

Ell linked her arm with Thad's and gave the other woman a friendly but distant smile. "We really do have to go, but it was nice meeting you. Let us know if we can help." She propelled Thad forward before Bambi could say another word.

"Not exactly remaining low profile there, Severance," she said in a low tone.

"I agree. Of all the people to bump into, that was the one person I did not need to see right now."

Ell risked a fast glance behind them. "It's all right, she's gone now." She turned back in time to see the sign for the street they wanted. "This way."

It was amazing how much could change in just a kilometer in a compact city like this one. One moment, they were off the strip yet clearly still in the gaming sector; the next, they were in the residential area. The farther in they went, the more opulent the homes.

The map Katie had made for them floated as a transparent overlay over Ell's optical implant; now it blinked at her to let her know they were nearing their destination.

{Oh my God…} she sent to Thad over the team channel. *{Dacina, was right about the gardens being a show place.}*

{Yeah, wow, right?} Micah's voice came over the channel. *{We're walking around the back side now. What took you guys so long?}*

{Later,} Thad said. *{Dacina's intel says the guests at tomorrow's party will be restricted to the garden. That ought to make things easier. Security will be focused outward, not inward. You found a good place for a sniper's hide yet?}*

For answer, Micah sent them the feed from his optics. Ell moved it to a floating window so she could see her own surroundings and what Micah saw at the same time.

She dropped two pins on the feed, one at the main door leading onto the terrace and one on the balcony above it. *{Dent is a true narcissist. He loves a grandiose entrance, all the attention it gets him. My money is on one of these two spots.}*

{I think you're right, cher, but if his security team is any good, they'll have a less obvious door nearby where they can hustle him back inside if things get rowdy—or if he just tires of it all.}

Micah's view shifted. *{Like this, you mean?}* he dropped a pin of his own onto a door partially obscured by a large flowering bush.

Dacina joined the conversation for the first time since leaving their rental. *{Your assessment, I believe, is accurate.}*

A notification that a file had been dropped into the channel popped up and Ell unpacked it. It contained snapshots of the drive leading to the service entrance and of the area inside the garden that was closest to it. *{This will be where catering sets up. There is a second hidden entrance nearby that mirrors the one Captain Case has identified. As soon as you can, slip inside.}*

{I can do that,} Ell said.

{I'll be roaming with Pascal,} Thad said. *{The moment we see Dent's team escorting him back in, we'll shadow them.}*

{I will be there as well. Captain Case?}

{Yes, Dacina?}

{Be ready to take out reinforcements.}

{I'll be ready.}

{Then you haul ass, hoss. We'll be at the door providing cover if you need it, but if everything goes as planned, you won't,} Thad said. *{We'll let you in, hustle Dent down to his ship, and sail away, nice and tidy.}*

There was a brief pause. *{I am surprised, Captain Severance,}* Dacina said. *{It seems someone has not read Sun Tzu.}*

TWELVE:
GARDEN PARTY

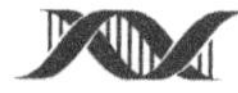

ASHER DENT'S RESIDENCE

At precisely 1600 local, Ell showed up dressed in the black suit and crisp white shirt the catering company required for its employees' attire. She was grateful they had specified a suit and not just a white shirt—it made weapons concealment much easier.

As Dacina's contact had warned them, there was an SI system on site. A scan was mandatory for all contracted labor entering the premises, but Dacina had said that their forged ID badges had been preloaded into the SI. If all went well, the system would not only ignore her; it would erase all record of her presence there.

She held her breath as the SI queried her ident, letting it out silently when it beeped green for the attending rent-a-cop, who waved her on.

Inside, she took a moment to walk around and get her bearings. It was good that they had solid visuals of the place—it helped them to build a rock-solid plan—but nothing beat boots on the ground. Walking around, getting a feel for distances. Target locations. Enemy head counts.

When the catering director rounded her up, somewhat exasperated that she'd gone walkabout, she apologized, telling the manager that she'd never seen the gardens before and wanted to get a feel for where she would be working.

{All set,} she told the team. *{Thad, how are you doing?}*

Based on his response, Thad was about five seconds away from losing his mind. *{If Pascal makes one more comment about sampling the local wildlife, I swear I'm going to shoot him.}*

{Pascal, give him a break, will you?} Micah said. *{Just look at him—the guy has zero sense of humor.}*

{I'm telling you, hoss, no judge would convict me.} Thad said. When he resumed, he was all business. *{I'm in position. I got us patrolling the perimeter near the target. I can see the hidden door. How 'bout you, Navy?}*

{I have eyes on the balcony and the terrace below—and I've deployed a couple of those new bots Colonel Valenti gave me before we left. They've hacked the security diffraction that keeps folks from seeing inside, so I have a clear view of what's going on in the house. The minute I see him on approach, I'll give the heads-up.}

{Dacina?} Ell asked.

{I am here.}

Ell waited a beat for the assassin to continue, but there was nothing. And then the catering manager was at her elbow, directing her to the tall, multi-shelved maglev rack that had just been pulled from the kitchen, laden with serving trays.

She grabbed one and moved out into the small clutch of guests that had arrived, the number growing by the minute. She functioned on autopilot, pausing with a practiced smile where people stood in twos and threes, to offer whatever was on the platter she carried.

Thank goodness the platter came with a holographic sign. It freed her from questions or other distractions, allowing her to focus on the mission. She worked her way around until she was in front of the flowering bush that hid the door. Just in time, too.

{He's coming. Terrace, not balcony.}

That was a relief. Now they wouldn't have to make it up to the second story and fight their way down *two* flights of stairs to get underground. Ell gave her surroundings a careful visual sweep; when no one was looking her way, she stepped quickly behind the bush.

{I'm going in,} she told them.

There was no response. She checked the signal. As they suspected might happen, it was being jammed. Ell was the only one truly out of comms range though; the rest could communicate through the chiral connections. She paused a moment to assess. Up until comms blackout, things were going exactly as planned, with everyone in position. She saw no reason not to proceed.

She shoved the now-empty platter beneath a bush, then, with another quick glance around, placed her palm over the door's access plate and activated the LockPik app stored in her implant's data partition. With a quiet *snick*, the door opened, swinging silently inward. She slipped inside.

The next part of her job called for clearing a path from the terrace to the basement. She stripped out of her waiter's costume, revealing the drakeskin suit she wore beneath it. She pulled her balaclava over her head and activated the suit's camouflage, then unholstered her CUSP and checked its charge. The compact, ultra-short pulse pistol was locked to her biosig—a handy thing in close quarters battle. It prevented the enemy from using a soldier's weapon against them if disarmed.

She cleared the first two rooms, sending tiny sniffer drones aloft to detect defensive systems built into the walls. The drones alerted her whenever one was found, then deployed a web of colloidene nano that reflected back a pattern to the defensive sensor that tricked the system into thinking the area was undisturbed.

The third one was trickier, as there was a small team of security standing at the bank of windows, weapons held at the ready. They were aimed outside, though, covering any potential threats that might arise from the guests.

Ell tested her bad leg, praying that it would hold if the need came to get the heck out of Dodge. There was no pain—but then again there never was… until there was. Or until the damn thing went out from under her completely. The last thing she needed right now was to take a tumble. Audio chaff might cover the fall, but not the vibration of her body hitting the ground. Or the wall.

Hoping for the best—and resolutely ignoring the voice inside her head that sounded suspiciously like her old drill instructor, reminding her that hope is not a plan—she popped chaff and crept along the room's perimeter, seeking the door that would lead down to Dent's hangar bay.

Her heart stopped when one of the bodyguards swung around, pointing his rifle inward. It started beating again when he complained to his partner, "Damn magazine's stuck again."

"Yeah? I swear, for all his talk about enemies going after him, this guy sure likes to outfit us with shitty munitions," the other one said in a tone that spoke of boredom. "How much longer is he going to mingle with them before Gus and Jay hustle him back inside?"

"Don't know, don't care. Once he's around the corner, he's their problem, not ours. As long as some whack job doesn't go loco out there and pull a pulse pistol in the next half hour, our job here's pretty much done."

That was good intel. Too bad Ell couldn't pass it along to anyone. Based on what she'd just heard, it sounded like they'd guessed correctly; Dent would do a fast fade from his own party out the side door.

Ell resumed her search for the basement door. By her estimate, about fifteen minutes had passed since her comms had gone on the fritz. She worked her way past the room's midpoint, and peeked into a corridor that led down one wing of the expansive home.

The nearest door was cracked open. In the dim lighting beyond, she could just make out a set of stairs leading downward Before she had a chance to investigate, she felt something bump into her from behind.

And then it began to crawl up her leg.

THIRTEEN:
BETRAYAL

Ell twisted, ready to brush off the offending creature—and came nose to nose with Sneaky Pete. Next, an invisible hand landed atop her arm. The physical connection established a closed, peer-to-peer connection. Of course it was Katie; it had to be.

{What happened to you staying back and monitoring?} Ell demanded before the pilot could speak.

{We're in a comms blackout. I'm not of much use to anyone if you can't hear what I'm reporting.}

{You got here too fast for that to be the case.}

{I heard chatter that they were going to be scrambling and hauled ass over here, okay? Figured I'd hook up with you, since you're the only one without a way to reach the others.}

That made good tactical sense. *{Can you get Sneaky Pete to check in with the others? I think I've found the door that leads to the hangar bay.}*

{Will do. What next?}

{I'm going down to recon the area. You stay up here and keep an

eye on these guys.}

{Copy. Thad says they're on the move.}

That was fast. Almost too fast. *{I'd better get moving then.}*

{Me too.}

Before Katie's words had time to register, the pilot moved away from Ell toward the window where the two armed guards still stood.

Ell raced after her and grabbed her arm. *{Katie! What the hell?}*

{I have all this ActiveFiber, and I'm itching to get rid of it. Think I'll set a few traps for these jokers. That'll be two less we need to worry about when the fur starts flying. Sneaky Pete, go with Ell. If Snotface has any news from Micah or Pascal, you tell her right away, okay?}

{O-kie dokie.}

Ell retreated slowly back to the stairs, debating the soundness of this plan. But Dacina had been right; Katie was very talented with ActiveFiber. Not only did she know how to spring traps on the unsuspecting, she knew how to do it in a way that looked utterly natural.

Good luck, she thought, then left Katie to her tricks and headed down to the mansion's lower level.

It didn't take long to recon the area. The hangar bay was simple and straightforward. The bay doors doubled as the landing pad; they opened outward, and the ship dropped down into the atmosphere. A yellow demarcation line clearly marked where the ES field would snap into place once the command to open the bay doors was entered into the console.

Ell applied a precautionary LockPik to the console so that once they had Dent in custody, the exfil could proceed smoothly. There really wasn't much else to the room, save for a small row of lockers that were installed against the far wall. She saw no secret door security could use to ambush them, and surprisingly, no defensive systems.

Satisfied that she'd done all she could to prep for a swift exit, Ell backtracked, Sneaky Pete pattering after her. The ferret was silent for once, maybe sensing the operation was nearing its critical moment.

Back on ground level, she hunted down Katie. *{Anything changed?}*

{Nope. Do me a favor and don't go past the hallway that dumps into the room from that side entrance, though, okay? You might trigger something you don't want to.}

{Copy that. I'm headed outside in case Thad needs back up.}

{I'm on your six, with Sneaky Pete.}

Ell slipped out the side door opposite the one she'd first entered, noting as she did that the sniffer drones had completed their work and all defensive systems were now neutralized. She spotted Thad immediately, dressed in the security company's vest that simply said SECURITY in bold letters across the back. Pascal was with him in a matching harness. It was attached to a leash Thad held, but everyone on the team recognized that for the fiction it was.

Thad was maneuvering around so that he'd be in position to slip in behind Dent's escort. Micah was hidden somewhere in the trees where he'd positioned himself as overwatch, joking on their way here that "you didn't do so well—you got me instead of Boone." By now, the pilot would probably be shimmying back down the tree, on his way to a rendezvous here at the side door.

She looked up into the trees anyway, trying to spot him. Her glance caught someone, another guard, standing on a low wall between her and Thad. This guard had his rifle out, too, like the ones in the house. Unlike the ones in the house, this one had his eye on the holographic reticle, actively trying to acquire a shot.

Ell followed his eyeline… back to Thad. *{Thad!}* she screamed mentally, even though she knew he couldn't hear. *{Pete! Tell Thad to get down! Pascal, sniper! Get down! Katie!}* Ell was babbling but she didn't care; she was too busy scrambling up the embankment that led to the wall and praying that her leg would hold.

As she closed, she realized she recognized this man from earlier that day. It was the same one in the hologram pendant Bambi wore. This was Ken, Thad's Marine buddy. His finger moved from the guard to the trigger, and she knew she wasn't going to make it in time.

Fear and blind rage coursed through her, stronger than anything she'd felt before. It lent her an almost inhuman strength. She unsheathed her knife and, with a guttural growl, sent it flying. The knife embedded itself hilt deep into his shoulder, and Ken's shot went wild.

Ell had lost her element of surprise, but she wasn't about to stop now. As Ken turned on her, years of training and kinetic memory kicked in. She put everything she had behind a vicious throat punch, aimed right at his Adam's apple. The SmartCarbyne reinforcing his body was the only thing that prevented his windpipe from being crushed, but it had to hurt like hell.

They went down hard, Ken taking advantage of his greater mass to flip her onto her back. That was fine by her; the action exposed the side of his neck. Fast as a striking snake, Ell tagged him with the ZipTie. The moment it connected with his bare skin, it isolated his wire, making it impossible for him to warn his cohort. It also immobilized him, seizing control of the web of SmartCarbyne nanofloss he'd been injected with prior to his first tour as a Marine.

Because she was still pissed as hell at his betrayal of an old friend, and because Ken was on top of her and she had to shove him off anyway, she shoved with both her hands *and* a vicious knee to the groin. She noted with a satisfaction the tears streaming from his eyes as he fell over onto his side.

She bent down, retrieved her blade, and whispered in one ear, "That's for betraying your old battle buddy, asshole."

She was sorely tempted to kick him in the kidney, had even drawn her foot back to deliver the blow, but then Dacina appeared from out of nowhere. "You let him live, I see. I would not have."

Ken's eyes grew a fraction wider, fear entering them as he registered the presence of an Akkadian assassin.

As if sensing his fear, and probably because she knew Ell well enough to feel the anger coming off her in waves, Dacina held a red bead up to the artificial sunlight. "I could do it for you."

The man at Ell's feet was crying again.

With a sigh, Ell shook her head. "Waste of a good bead. Come on, they're waiting for us."

FOURTEEN:
FIREFIGHT

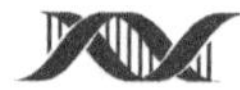

To Ell's surprise, the entire incident up on the wall had garnered no notice from anyone other than Dacina and the rest of the team. She and the assassin crouched on the berm adjacent to the side door, out of sight of the oncoming procession with Dent and his three guards. Sneaky Pete had once again found his way to Ell.

{Can you contact your twin on board Wraith? Micah and Pascal need to know that Katie set traps inside, and that all the defense systems have been neutralized. Can you do that?}

{Pffft. Katie blue-hair have silky traps, yes-yes. Bad stuff gone-gone. I get shiny now? Waitey, waitey, Micah say he see us.} The ferret stood up on his hind legs and waved wildly—to what, or where, Ell had no idea. *{Hiiiii Micah! Hi! Okay, Micah say bad-bad people inside now, it safe to come down.}*

Dacina's expression suggested that the ferret was giving her a headache. Without a word, she leapt nimbly down, then turned and looked expectantly back at Ell. "Are you coming?"

"Not the same way you did. I don't trust my bad leg not to give out on me."

"Try it," Dacina invited. "I think you will be surprised."

Ell rubbed her thigh and realized that she hadn't felt her leg twitch once throughout the op. That was a first since the explosion. She flashed back to the assassin's enigmatic response when she'd asked what the design on her leg would look like.

The needles know.

Ell wondered what else the assassin had done to her…

Taking a literal leap of faith, Ell jumped. And landed as lightly on her feet as she had countless times while serving as a sniper for the SRU. She shoved aside her shock. Now was not the time to question things; they had a mission to complete. She'd think about the implications later.

Ell jogged over to Thad and gripped his arm, establishing yet another peer-to-peer link to let him see her presence. "Ready?" she asked.

"To put this *couyon* down once and for all? Hell yes."

Out of habit, Ell nodded toward the house, though with her suit's active camo, Thad couldn't see her. "Katie's inside. She's setting traps throughout the main level to slow any pursuit. I think I saw some flash-bangs and sticky grenades in her hands before I came out."

As if her comment conjured the lanky pilot, signal interference dropped and their team channel came online.

{Score another one for the blue-haired wonder,} Micah said. *{Good job, Katie.}*

{Snares set at every entrance, and then some,} Katie warned them. *{Stick to the direct path between your entry point and the basement door and you should be fine. I'm already down here. I used the hangar bay's console to hack the house and disable the jammer. I'm going to tackle the security team's frequency next. If I can reverse it, they won't be able to communicate with each other, coordinate a counterattack, or call for reinforcements.}*

{Good thinking,} Ell said. *{Dent's team just hustled him inside. We're coming in behind them.}*

{Copy that,} Katie replied. *{I'll be waiting.}*

"All right, let's do this," Thad said as Micah joined them. "Ell, you and Dacina take point. Micah and I will cover your six."

He looked around to confirm the large hedge in front of the door concealed them from curious eyes, then stripped down to his drakeskin suit. Micah did the same, then wadded up their clothing and discarded it while Thad freed Pascal from his harness. The collar around the big cat's neck was the same as the one Sneaky Pete wore, technology ordinarily used to camouflage stationary buildings or vehicles from prying eyes.

As Thad had reminded Ell in the spaceport the day before, the tech wasn't so good when it came to hiding a moving object like a cat or a ferret. Its ability to conceal functioned much better in low light. But it was all they had.

"You two hug the walls," Thad told them. "Stay close behind us, and for God's sake, if bullets start flying, get low to the ground. You hear me?"

The big cat growled.

{Pascal say we not deaf,} Sneaky Pete helpfully interpreted.

"Yeah, I got that." Thad scowled at Pascal, lowered his balaclava and vanished.

Dacina was already at the door, waiting for them. "*Bad ba shoma ba shed,*" she murmured as Ell slipped in behind her. It was the traditional Akkadian farewell-into-battle, "May the winds be with us."

Ell felt a slight breeze as Micah closed the door behind the animals, saw a brief flash as he used his P-SCAR to ensure that no one followed them inside.

{Twenty meters to your left is a hallway that leads to the main living area,} Ell told them. *{Access to the basement is just before the corridor ends.}*

Katie cut in. *{You'd better get down here. Footsteps and voices are coming this way—and they're not yours.}*

{Katie, get behind the console, now!} Ell ordered. *{It's not much, but hopefully it'll do for concealment until we get there.}*

{Hey, why would Dent be heading down to the hangar bay?}
Micah asked. *{Did something tip him off?}*

{Possibly,} Ell said. *{We didn't have access to the gardens ahead of time.}*

That was the big weak spot in their plan. The file Dacina's contact had given them was thin on information pertaining to the gardens. Dent could have had defensive systems installed that they could not detect.

Ell was sure their covers had held, otherwise they wouldn't have been permitted to enter in the first place. But Dent would recognize Dacina and Ell on sight—and know they were after him.

{Remember the assassination attempt on Coalition leaders during the summer hosted on Hawking?} she asked.

{Kind of hard to forget when the weapon they used was a chirally entangled virus.} There was real anger in Micah's voice. *{And the people behind it were the ones who kidnapped Sam.}*

Thad added, *{Yeah, I remember. Dent was Premier of Akkadia at the time. He was one of the people targeted. We actually thought he was one of the good guys back then.}*

{Yeah, well, I was there when Dent learned about the plot. Dacina was, too. He knows us both by sight. It's possible he IDed me when I arrived. If so…}

They were interrupted by a loud crash.

FIFTEEN:
CHECKMATE

BASEMENT
ASHER DENT'S RESIDENCE

On the heels of the crash came the unmistakable sound of a flash-bang. That was Katie's work. The sound of thrashing and loud curses brought a pair of guards out of a nearby room. They raced to their teammates' aid, feet thudding on the thick carpeted pile.

"Rieger, Siemens!" one of them called out. "Report!"

A voice in the distance yelled, "Intruders! Comms are jammed, switch to lo-band!"

"Lo-band!" one of the ones running yelled over his shoulder.

A figure appeared in the open door. "Lo-band, copy." She looked both ways down the hall, a calculating look coming over her face, then she disappeared back into the room. When she came back out, she had a small device in her hand. She tossed it down the corridor in their direction.

{*What the—?*} Micah asked.

Ell and Thad responded just as the device exploded midair into a cloud of tiny glittering flecks. {*Colloid mist.*}

{Damn. That'll cling to our stealth suits. There goes our concealment.}

Dacina was already on the move. One of her daggers went flying, embedding itself in the woman's neck. With a surprised look, she went down, clutching her throat.

Ell dove beneath the cloud to minimize the amount of glittery colloids that stuck to her. Dacina somersaulted over it. Micah went high, using the organogel in his gloves and boots to crabwalk past on the ceiling. With Thad's mass, there was no avoiding the stuff, so he just plowed straight through the center of it.

The downed guard hadn't been alone. Another guard popped out of the door and fired a round at Thad. She pulled back inside when he and Micah returned fire and another of Dacina's daggers embedded itself in the door jamb.

{Okay, now I'm mad,} Thad said.

With comms reestablished, Ell now had access to the team's suit telemetry; a yellow ring showed where the bullet had grazed Thad's thigh, though the drakeskin diffused and absorbed much of it. She crossed in front of the door in a combat crouch, firing her CUSP in three-burst rounds as she went. Her HUD showed the area inside the room to be clear.

Micah sent a microdrone flying through the door. *{There are three of them. Two are hiding on either side of the entrance. A third is in the back, behind an overturned table. Stand back.}* He brought his P-SCAR around from where it had been slung over his shoulder and, using the drones as a remote aiming device, fired through the wall, first on one side and then the other in rapid succession.

Ell had positioned herself to approach from one side; Dacina mirrored her actions. They moved in sync, entering the room one after the other, Pascal on their heels.

Ell double-tapped the guard on the left and decided not to turn and look when she heard another blade sing as Dacina drew it from its scabbard. With a feral snark, Pascal leapt over the table. An aborted scream was followed by the grating of bone on bone as the hunting cat snapped the third guard's neck.

{He was going to shoot me.}

Ell didn't doubt that.

{Contact! We need to get out of this hallway, it's a kill box,} Micah said. More gunfire erupted, and then there was the snap of a large electrical discharge, and the weapons exchange stopped, replaced by shrieks of pain.

Ell raced out of the room, her CUSP leading the way. Micah was still high; Thad was at the end of the hallway by the basement door. On the floor beyond them, where the hallway spilled out into the main room, two men were down. One was unconscious; the other frozen in a rictus of pain, his hand wrapped around a strand of ActiveFiber that was active in more than one sense.

{How the hell did Katie string that wire without electrocuting herself in the process?} Ell wondered, careful to avoid touching the man. Then she dipped inside the door and started down the stairs.

{Hey! Who said you were going first, cher?}

{All the glitter crap marking you as a big, fat easy target,} she said, popping another cloud of audio chaff. She sent one of the crawler recon drones down ahead of her, sharing its feed on the team channel.

It showed Dent at the row of lockers, pulling out an object that looked like one of those portable Tau-Neu stasis units Ell had seen Sam use in her lab.

Three more guards were stationed around the room. One was at the demarcation line, as if ready to defend against incursions coming from outside. Predictably, the other two were stationed on either side of the stairs, weapons pointed up at the treads disappearing into the ceiling.

The stairs were open, with railings on either side. The fact they weren't against a wall meant there was no easy way for Ell or the others to descend without using the steps. Unless…

Ell silently eased her way back up. *{I have an idea. Sneaky Pete, how comfortable would you be taking the railing down instead of the stairs?}*

The ferret's approach was barely noticeable, just a slight ripple of deformation against the wall. A person had to know what they were looking for—or be exceptionally observant—to realize he was there. He crept past Ell and peered down at the stairs. When she felt his paws on her leg, she knelt.

{Railing easy-peasey. No likey mans at bottom though. They smell bad.}

{Can you get down there though?}

{Yessy yes. Then what?}

That was the ten thousand credit question. Ell brought up the crawler's feed. *{Do you see those canisters on that bench lining the far wall? Think you can run past them and knock them all to the ground?}*

{I not get in trouble?} Sneaky Pete sounded doubtful.

{No trouble,} she assured him. *{Katie's trapped down there with the bad men and we need to get her out. This will help Katie.}*

{O-kie dokie. I go now.}

Thad had come up behind her. He dropped a pin on one of the two tangos below. *{I'll take this guy. You take the other. Micah, you're on number three by the bay doors. Dacina— Where's Dacina?}*

The assassin had disappeared.

{Crap. Katie, you okay covering Dent?}

{On it.}

They crept down as far as they could without being exposed and waited for Sneaky Pete. The moment the clattering began, Ell launched herself down the stairs, firing as she went.

The guards were well-trained. One of them kept his weapon aimed up the stairs while the other swept the barrel of his gun around in an arc, seeking the intruder. With Thad no longer camouflaged, he took most of the fire, but one of the bullets winged Ell's face close enough for her suit to register it as a graze.

She took the last few steps the fast way, sliding down the railing feet first, her boots plowing into the tango's chest. He went down and she leapt over him, pivoting fast to drill three CUSP shots into her opponent—two in the chest and one in the head.

The room fell silent, save for the slow sound of someone clapping. It came from Asher Dent.

SIXTEEN:
CHIRAL

BASEMENT
ASHER DENT'S RESIDENCE

"I see you found me, Agent Cyr. Well done. Well done indeed."

The mocking tone in Dent's voice made Ell want to rip out his throat with her bare hands.

"And the figure looming over me right now would be Captain Severance, am I right? Where is your chiral pet?"

A low growl emitted from the foot of the stairs.

"Ah, the hunting cat has joined the party. Which one is this, the original or the clone?"

Thad, his CUSP leveled at Dent, jerked his balaclava free and triggered his suit back to its standard urban-camo pattern. "You talk a good game for a man who is about to be hauled before a Coalition court. What are you hoping to accomplish, a little frontier justice?"

"No, Captain. And as much as I would enjoy the enchanting Miss Cyr's company—and the young woman glowering at me from behind the console… Katie Hyer, am I right? I really must decline."

{What the hell's he talking about?} Micah asked.

But Ell was staring at the Tau-Neu chamber Dent held in his hand. She was getting a sinking feeling she knew where this was leading.

She pulled her own balaclava free and advanced on him, her weapon moving from him to the chamber. "Set it down, nice and easy." When he didn't move, she thumbed the CUSP, taking it to its highest setting. It whined as it moved to full charge. "That was not a request."

"I'm sure it wasn't," he said pleasantly. "But don't you want to ask me first what's inside?"

"We're done playing games, Dent," Micah growled, stepping in front of Ell and reaching for the chamber.

"Ah-ah-ah! No handling the merchandise, Case. Not until you have a chance to talk to Doctor Travis about its contents."

Micah froze at his mention of Sam.

"Ah, *now* I have your attention." Dent turned to Katie. "Excellent work, hacking my home's system, by the way."

"All right, I'll bite. What's in the box?" Katie asked.

"A vial. A rather deadly one, I'm afraid. I was curious about the virus my enemies had created to eliminate me and the rest of the Coalition leaders on Hawking, so I instructed Clint Janus to recreate it. Unfortunately, you got to him before he could mass produce it. Just this single vial remains."

Dread crashed through Ell like a cyclone. That virus had been engineered to spread rapidly, the death rate among the infected impossibly high.

Dent smiled, an oily, ugly, *satisfied* smile. "Your expression betrays you, Agent Cyr. You're horrified that I would do such a thing? I assure you, I have no intention of releasing it—if you let me go." He raised the chamber to eye level and studied it admiringly. "A modified Sargon virus, encapsulated in a single, perfect chiral supraparticle. Entangled with its non-chiral twin, somewhere on Illuminari. Somewhere you cannot possibly reach in time."

"He's bluffing," Micah growled.

Dent lifted a brow. "Am I? Try me. You let me onto my ship and I give Agent Cyr this stasis box." He turned it so that they could see the device adhered to its backside, then he lifted his free hand. Clutched in it was another device.

{*Dead man's switch,*} Thad told them.

{*Yeah, my thinking, too.*} Micah said.

Dent was smiling again. Ell really, really hated that smile. "The chamber is keyed to your biosig, Agent Cyr. I wouldn't try to unlock it until I'm out of range or those explosives *will* detonate."

"Why hers? And how did you get her biosig?" Thad demanded.

"She's a profiler. And she befriended a Tèzhŏng. She knows I mean what I say. As for the DNA…" For the first time, Dent's façade cracked, and he showed real anger. "Did you really think you could infiltrate *my home* without my knowledge?"

Ell decided to poke him a bit more, get him to lose enough control that he got sloppy. Give them an opportunity to neutralize the switch in his hand. "Big talk from a guy who's now no more than a two-bit underworld smuggler. How far you've fallen, Asher Dent."

It didn't work; Dent saw through it, she could tell. He gave her a sad, condescending look. "You don't believe me? Perhaps you would like to confirm that with the lovely Doctor Travis." He turned to Katie. "My dear, if you would be so kind as to contact the NSA on Ceriba? I'm sure you noticed I have direct, private access to Venus's Starshot constellation. Perk of the business."

Katie looked questioningly at Thad. As mission leader, this was his call. He nodded for her to go ahead. Katie worked the console and a holoscreen flickered into existence, floating above the workstation. It bore the NSA's crest.

Seconds later, an SI answered. "You have reached the Geminate National Security Agency. How may I direct your call?"

Dent raised his voice so that it carried clearly over to the console. "Doctor Samantha Travis, please. Tell her Asher Dent wishes to speak with her. And that Micah Case is with him."

"One moment." The line fell silent, the sigil rotating slowly on the screen.

"This can't be real," Micah murmured softly.

Ell knew what he meant. This whole situation had a sense of unreality about it. But if Dent was telling the truth, and she sensed that he was…

"I think it is. He's just that arrogant. He's a grandiose narcissist, and this is his stage."

"Profiling again, Agent Cyr? Brava."

{Thad, if he's not lying and that stasis field fails, millions could die.}

Thad acknowledged Ell's unspoken words with a slight nod. *{Yeah, I know. Us included, cher. Micah's the only one who would survive. His chiral physiology gives him immunity. Him and Pascal.}*

Just then, Sam appeared on screen. She looked winded and tense, like she'd raced to get to the console where she stood. There were no identifying objects behind her, just a neutral background. The wait had been long enough that Ell suspected a lot more eyes were on this than just Sam's.

"What do you want, Dent?" Sam demanded.

"Merely to have you confirm what I just told your colleagues." He recapped everything he'd said to Ell and the others, adding in more scientific detail that was above Ell's pay grade.

Sam visibly whitened. "Yes, he's correct," she said. "If we agree to this, you will tell us where the other vial is?"

"No, Doctor Travis. I don't believe I will. Thank you for verifying. Good day."

"Wait! Micah, be careful with it—it's dangerou—" Her voice cut off as Dent terminated the call remotely, yet another indication that he was stage directing this whole scene, and that he saw Ell and her teammates as players to be manipulated at his whim.

"Now, where were we? Ah yes." He set the chamber down on the bench behind him and straightened, his fist held high, clenching the dead man's switch. "I'd like to say it's been a pleasure, but now I'm going to have to rebuild somewhere else."

Ell caught a flicker of movement behind Dent, the flash of a blade leaving concealment. And then it was gone.

She knew instantly what the assassin planned. *{We need to stall him! Dacina's edging around him to get inside that ship.}*

Ell stepped forward. "Hold on, how do we even know that box is coded to me?" She injected disdain into her tone, and a healthy dose of skepticism. "You act as if you see all, know all, but you really expect us to believe you had time to obtain my DNA and set all this up since we arrived? Right. Pull the other one, asshole."

Dent turned to face Ell, his attention entirely on her. "My, so hostile. You want proof? Fine. Pick up the box."

"Don't do it, Ell," Thad warned.

Ell side-stepped around Dent, forcing him to turn his back to where she approximated Dacina's location was. When her knee bumped the bench, she looked down. The statis chamber was a cube about ten centimeters on each side. When she touched it, the device chirped and a green light on its front panel came online.

"Ell," Thad warned, his voice tight.

Katie looked over at the ship maglocked into position above the bay doors then looked quickly away. Ell didn't think Dent saw. She was also certain Dacina had somehow signaled the young pilot. With Dent focused on her, she didn't dare chance a look for herself.

Then Katie moved. She rounded the console, comp unit in hand. When she was far enough away from the ship's sightline, she called out, "Let me scan it first, Ell." She was careful to cross behind both Micah and Thad, to not spoil their aim.

Ell shifted, ostensibly toward the approaching Katie. The move was deliberate, though, and she stopped when the ship was directly behind Dent. She fixed her stare on Dent but let her gaze defocus slightly. And there it was, another flash, and movement as the ship's hatch swung silently closed once more—with Dacina inside.

SEVENTEEN:
BOOBY TRAPPED

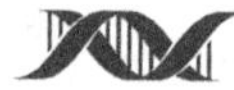

"He's right. It's biolocked to you," Katie said, stepping back.

Ell gestured to the ship. "Fine, Dent. You win this round. But you knew that already."

"That you wouldn't sacrifice the lives of innocents in your pursuit of me?" Dent laughed and backed toward the ship. "I'm afraid that didn't take much to figure out. The thing in your hands, on the other hand, is a work of art." He cycled the hatch open, stepped inside, then paused, his hand on the door panel. "Or as I like to call it, performance art."

The door shut and a few seconds later, the bay's ES field snapped into place, signaling the hangar doors were about to open.

"She made it inside, right? Dacina?" Micah asked.

"Yes. She signaled me while Katie scanned the box."

"No," the assassin countered, stepping out from concealment. "There was room only for one. But I planted a tracker."

"Damn, I was hoping you'd gutted the weasel and jettisoned his entrails," Micah said. "There aren't too many people I say this about but Dent's completely irredeemable. A waste of good oxygen."

"Ooh-rah," Thad replied, in full agreement with his assessment.

"Now, what are we going to do with this thing?" Ell asked.

Thad's eyes were on the ship, which dropped through the open hole and out of sight. The bay doors were still open, and they could see the clouds of sulfuric acid churning below. "Why don't we just eject the whole thing? Let Venus's atmosphere destroy it?"

"Not while the vial's still inside that chamber. There's no guarantee that it wouldn't trigger the vial before it burns up," Sam's voice said from the console.

"Sam? I thought Dent cut you off," Micah said.

"He did." Katie said. "I reconnected. Hang tight." She did something with the console and Sam's face reappeared.

"Okay, doc, tell us what to do," Thad said.

Sam moved aside and Boone, the team's sniper and explosives expert, stepped into the picture. "Bring it closer so I can see it. And Katie, shoot me the results of that scan."

A few tense minutes passed. For some reason, Ell was afraid to set the chamber down, so she held it. It was funny how something that weighed so little could grow so heavy over time.

"Okay, Dent was telling the truth," Boone said. "If Ell presses on the lock, center front, her biosig will unlock it. But seal your suits first in case the vial ruptures."

"Let me do it," Micah suggested. "I'm the only one who's immune."

"No, it's coded to me. It has to be me."

Sam was back. "Okay Ell, do it, but carefully. Then pull the vial out."

"I'm going to have to set this down to seal my suit."

"Here, let me."

Thad held the chamber while Ell sealed her suit—leaving only her hand exposed for biometrics.

"You good?" he asked.

"Five by five," Ell said. She looked around to make sure everyone else was suited up, then took a deep breath. "Okay, here goes."

Thad had positioned himself across from her, his hands cupped beneath the Tau-Neu chamber in case anything happened. Dacina stood beside him. Over her HUD, she saw Thad's green-outlined form give her a nod. It was time.

She pressed her thumb against the lock, initiating a handshake between the biosig stored in her suit and the chamber's security system. The chamber vibrated and lit up. Then, with a loud *snick*, needles shot out of its base, stabbing Ell's hand.

Reflexively, she flinched. "Ow!"

Thad grabbed the chamber by its sides and set it on the bench. "I knew it! I knew he was up to something. Micah, Katie, secure the vial." Then he was back with Ell, his hands gentle as they examined her palm. "Sam, the chamber was rigged. Ell's been stabbed by some needle-like device in the chamber's base."

Sneaky Pete pattered up to her and reared onto his hind legs, patting her leg urgently with his paws. *{Ell smell wrong! Ell smell wrong!}*

She was beginning to feel woozy—no surprise, the needles had to have been laced with something.

"I have the vial," Micah said. "Sam, what do I do with it?"

"Vaporize it. Use your P-SCAR. Highest setting." Sam's voice sounded as if it was coming from a great distance.

"Hand me that stasis box!" Dacina snapped. Micah handed it over, then carefully set the vial down on the reinforced bay doors, the plating rated to resist a ship's plasma burn.

Ell felt weirdly disconnected from her body. Her gaze drifted lazily back to Dacina. Was she *sniffing* the needles?

"Poison," the assassin said., shoving the box into Katie's hands and heading for the stairs. "You need to get her to Akkadia, now."

"Where do you think you're going?" Thad asked.

"After Dent." She paused on the first step. "Ask for Che Josza. Tell him I sent you. And show him the mark on her leg."

Then she was gone.

Ell's eyes wanted to close. She was having a difficult time forming words. "I'm feeling…"

Then the darkness claimed her.

When Ell awoke, she was in a strange environment. The room smelled like a hospital, but also not. An unusual scent floated on the air. She blinked up at the ceiling, memory coming slowly back to her.

Dent. The party. Infiltrating his home. The Tau-Neu chamber. *The chamber.*

She tried to sit up, but hands pressed her back down into the bed. A face came into view. He was Akkadian. And she knew him.

"You were poisoned, do you remember?" Che Josza asked.

Ell licked her lips, wondering why in the hell the Akkadian Minister of State Security was in her hospital room—and what that meant for her recovery. She tried to speak. It came out as a croak.

"Apologies. They said you would want water when you awoke." He disappeared, to return with a cup filled with ice and what looked like water.

Ell stared at the cup in his hand. Her brain was still coming online. Should she take what he offered? Was it drugged? Some kind of trick? She fought for clarity, the questions hammering at her.

She'd waited too long to respond. Josza's brows twitched in concern before his expression cleared.

"Ah. It is safe, I assure you." He took a sip from the cup, then handed it to her. "See?"

"Thank you," she whispered.

He touched a button and the head of her bed lifted so that she was sitting up.

That's when she discovered that Josza hadn't come alone. "Premier Enlai," Ell said. She looked from one to the other, then around at her room again, this time through new eyes. "I'm on Akkadia."

Rin Zhou Enlai inclined her head regally, the only acknowledgement Ell received to her statement.

"What happened?"

Che chuckled. "Ah, now there's a story we must savor over coffee. For now, our doctors have ordered you to rest and recover. Sleep. We will speak of this later."

EIGHTEEN:
AUDIENCE

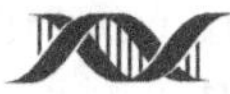

PREMIER'S CHAMBERS
CENTRAL PREFECTURE
ERIDU, AKKADIA

When Ell awoke again she felt much better, but she had a desperate need to use the facilities. Though she was alone in her room, she had little doubt that she was being monitored. She was, after all, an agent working for a foreign nation.

The fact she helped overthrow Dent on their own soil while working alongside Dacina and her sister warriors, the ones known as the Dagger's Dozen, was probably the only reason she was in a hospital room and not restrained in a cell.

The small lav was clearly marked. When she returned, Che was waiting for her—confirmation that she was, indeed, being watched.

"It is gratifying to see you moving about," he said.

Ell walked carefully back to the bed, using the movement to stall for time, and to take mental inventory of her condition. Weak. Fatigued despite the hours she'd spent asleep, her body fighting whatever poison Dent had coated those needles with, in his sick game. She wasn't exactly in fighting trim, but she could run if the need arose.

She decided to get straight to the point. "Please pardon my bluntness, but why are you treating me like a guest and not a..."

The Akkadian's brow lifted. "Not an enemy operative?" He gestured and Ell noticed for the first time that he carried a pile of clothes, neatly folded. "Get dressed, and we will speak. Is this, as you say, a deal?"

She took them gratefully. "Yes, Citizen Minister. It's a deal."

He stepped out of the room to give her privacy. She shed her hospital garb and changed quickly into the pants and shirt he had provided. Her hands smoothed the fabric as she faced herself in the mirror. The outfit looked similar to ones she'd seen Dacina wearing. She looked surreptitiously around for anything that she might be able to slip up her sleeve to use as a weapon if it came to that, but the Akkadians had done a good job of clearing out the room.

Might as well get on with it, then, she thought. She approached the door, half expecting to be locked in. It slid open silently. Che was there, waiting.

"Shall we?" He gestured down the hall.

She fell into step beside him. "Where am I?"

"As you so astutely guessed, you are on Akkadia. You were treated in the Citizens' Clinic and then transferred here, to the Premier's private medical suite." He glanced at her. "A high honor."

That was the last thing Ell had expected to hear. She didn't know what to say to that, so she changed the subject. "My friends who brought me in..."

"Have been docked at the trade station in orbit. They are on their way down now."

"Ah." The mystery deepened. This felt a little bit like some of the state department visits she'd been assigned when she'd been with the Unit, only instead of working protective detail for the person visiting, the tables had been flipped. *She* was the visitor.

Che led her down a second corridor, then stopped in front of an ornate door. "The protocol here is to enter and remain at a respectful distance, not speaking until acknowledged."

"I understand."

"Good." He signaled whoever was inside. Moments later, the door slid open and a servant bowed. "Citizen Minister. The Premier awaits you."

He stepped aside and Che entered, Ell on his heels. The servant bowed himself out, sealing the door behind them. Ell followed Che's cues; she copied his stance, his folded hands, and remained silent beside him, head down. Out of the corner of her eyes, though, she was watching. And curious.

She'd absorbed a lot during that first fast look she'd taken when they entered. The room struck her as a contradiction. It was spare, with very little in the way of furnishings. Yet what was there seemed… ornate. The walls were lined with real wood paneling that looked like it had been imported from Earth by the first colonists. The furnishings were elegant. They also looked ancient.

"Citizen Minister, approach. And bring our esteemed guest with you."

A sidelong look at Che told Ell that it was okay to lift her head. She met Rin Zhou's eyes and nodded respectfully, then followed behind Che as he approached the Premier's desk.

Rin Zhou fixed her gaze first on Che. "Our guests have arrived?"

"Yes, Premier. They are being escorted to the receiving room as we speak."

"Excellent. And you, Elodie Cyr. The marking on your leg proclaims you as a sister to my Tèzhǒng. This is an honor few receive. It is not, however, the reason why you were accepted into the Citizens' Clinic. That we would have done anyway, as repayment for your part in hunting down Asher Dent."

"And we let him go," Ell said bitterly.

"That you did."

Ell wondered if she was about to see the other shoe drop. It would be very Akkadian to give with one hand, while taking away with the other.

"The bastard was holding an entire city hostage. Millions of people. I had no choice."

"We always have choices, Elodie Cyr." Rin Zhou inclined her head in that way that neither agreed nor disagreed with that decision. "Be that as it may, you assisted the Citizen Minister's Dagger. This will not be forgotten."

Che's Dagger? Ell abruptly recalled the closeness she'd sensed when she'd seen the two together, back on Hawking. And again, how protective Dacina had been of him during their raid on the Shar-Kali Correctional Facility in Akkadia's Aksu Desert—the place where Dent had held captive some of the leaders from other star nations. Where he carried out his plans to create and enslave their clones.

She glanced over at Che for confirmation. "Dacina?" she asked.

There was no mistaking the fondness in Che's eyes. "Yes. Her given name is Dacina Zian."

"Fierce Dagger," Ell translated, abruptly realizing that it must have been Josza who had given her the name. "It's fitting."

"I thought so."

Rin Zhou gestured to a door inset into the back of the room. "Your team awaits you, Elodie Cyr. Let us not keep them waiting."

NINETEEN:
HEAD ON A PIKE

RECEIVING ROOM
STATE ASSEMBLY HOUSE
ERIDU, AKKADIA

The door led to a secret passageway. *How very clandestine*, Ell thought as she followed the Premier, Che bringing up the rear. This was by design, she was sure. If she made any attempt to threaten Rin Zhou, Che would not hesitate to shoot her in the back.

The tunnel smelled old and musty and was dimly lit, but the walk itself was brief. Within minutes, they were exiting into an anteroom every bit as ancient and formal as Rin Zhou's office.

The servants that greeted them bowed respectfully. The one in charge stepped forward. "Your guests are seated, Madam Premier, and the service is ready."

"Excellent. Have them bring it in immediately." Rin Zhou moved now with purpose, striding toward the door, which slid open at her approach.

The murmur of voices that came from within stopped abruptly

at her entrance. Then Ell was through the door and staring into faces both familiar and beloved.

The relief in Thad's eyes was palpable. She could almost feel the once-over he gave her, searching for signs of injury or ill-treatment. She flashed him a hand signal: *all okay.*

He flashed her a smile, white teeth in a dusky face. "El-o-die," he drawled. "Been sleeping the day away, I hear."

Screw propriety, she thought, and stepped close. Thad's arms opened and she walked into them, enveloped in a hug so strong, it telegraphed both his fear and his love.

"Don't scare me like that again, *cher*," he whispered softly into her hair. "Promise?"

Ell's throat clogged. She resisted the urge to stay sheltered within the arms of this man, a man who had become so dear to her. The reasons she'd used to justify holding him at arms' length, despite how they both felt—fraternization, her injury, conflict of interest, her injury—seemed pointless now.

Realization struck hard. She'd been so afraid to saddle him with a 'broken Ell' that she'd been subconsciously pushing him away, despite his assurances that it did not matter. But whatever Dacina had done seemed to have made her whole again. The how and the why of that was still a mystery to her.

A throat cleared loudly behind her. "Dude, gonna give the rest of us a chance here?"

She felt his kiss on the top of her head, the lightest brush of his lips, then he released her and stepped back.

Micah favored her with a lopsided grin. "You keep doing this, you know. Getting injured by Akkadians. I'm not sure this planet is good for your health."

She slugged him lightly in the arm.

"Haven't you heard?" Che said mildly. "The Akkadian atmosphere is not good for *anyone's* health."

Katie peered out from behind Micah, Pascal pressing close against her. "Did he just make a joke? Because I swear he made a joke."

Rin Zhou swept out a hand to indicate a seating area in a recessed section of the room. "Please. Join me for coffee."

Micah waggled his brows silently at Ell, and they turned to follow. The table was low, the seats were ornate pillows encircling it. Ell waited for the Premier to indicate where she wished each person to sit, then waited for Che to cue them.

Rin Zhou lowered herself gracefully into a lotus position, a feat Ell knew it would be impossible to emulate. She did the best she could when Che indicated which pillow was hers.

Pascal settled in beside her and, with a chuff, laid his head in her lap. A small gob of spittle splashed onto her arm, and she surreptitiously wiped it away. Maybe not so surreptitiously, she realized, when she heard Thad's mental laugh.

{Better you than me, cher. Better you than me.}

Once they were all seated, Rin Zhou lifted a silver mallet and struck a small silver disc floating vertically on a maglev pedestal. The disc was engraved with Akkadian symbols Ell could not read.

The response was immediate. The door opened to admit a trio of servants pushing a cart laden with carafes, cups, and other objects she couldn't identify.

"Are you familiar with the traditional Akkadian coffee ceremony?" Che asked.

"No sir, I'm afraid I'm not," Thad told him.

"Then you are in for a treat."

The barista carefully weighed out a mound of glistening black coffee beans while the other two delivered cups and saucers to each seated person. Ell instinctively stiffened when the barista reached for something on a lower shelf, but the item she returned with was nothing more threatening than a hand grinder.

She ground the beans into a fine powder, then presented them to the Premier, who waved a hand over it on a slow inhale. Rin Zhou nodded her approval, and the barista retreated to her cart where she divided the grounds into smaller portions. She then began a gentle, rhythmic pour of heated water over the grounds. The slow, fluid weave of her hand was hypnotic. The aroma was heavenly.

"Mesmerizing, is it not?" Rin Zhou murmured.

Ell glanced over at her to find the Premier's eyes on her, not on the pour.

"It is," she agreed. "And if I'm permitted to say, it smells wonderful."

"A compliment to the bean is always appropriate."

Ell blinked but said nothing. While she appreciated a good cup as much as the next person, the formality of this ritual struck her as something just shy of religious fervor.

The server set the first cup in front of the Premier, then waited by her side while she cupped her hand around the rim.

"And now you breathe the bean," Rin Zhou explained. She bent her head and inhaled, long and slow, as if to capture every molecule of fragrance floating in the air around her. She held it for a long moment, then exhaled, nodding. "Excellent," she murmured. Her hand moved fluidly, clear instruction to serve the table.

The barista poured and the servers delivered. Ell and her teammates watched carefully as Che repeated the breathing thing, then it was their turn. Ell did the best she could, but by the pained look on Che's face, she knew she had a lot to learn before she could pass as an Akkadian.

And then she took her first sip.

"Oh wow," Katie said, awe in her tone. "This is nothing like the coffee Dacina made for us on Venus. This is *amazing*."

Ell caught Thad's wince and knew what he was thinking. A quick glance over at Rin Zhou, though, dispelled her fear that Katie had broken the ritual's protocol.

The Premier was beaming at Katie with genuine pleasure. "Now *this* one truly respects the bean."

The longer the ritual went on, the more Ell chafed; she had so many questions she wanted to ask.

Where was Dent? Did Dacina catch him? Did they neutralize the chiral virus before it triggered the release of its entangled twin?

But such discussion was not permitted, she could tell. Not over coffee. At long last, Rin Zhou signaled coffee was complete. She rang the silver gong once more; the barista and her two helpers cleared the table, stored their cart against the wall behind Rin Zhou—within the Premier's reach should she want another cup, or so Ell assumed—then departed.

Ell waited impatiently for the door to close after them. Then the words spilled from her mouth. "Where is Dacina?"

That surprised her; it wasn't at all the first question she'd intended to ask. But now that it was out there, she realized she'd grown concerned for the assassin.

Che gave Rin Zhou a look that said *I told you so.*

"She is well," he said. "She is on another mission. But she wished for you to know that she found Asher Dent."

"Good," Ell said. "We were sent to bring him in for trial. We failed. I'd like a chance to rectify that. If she needs help…" Her voice trailed off when Rin Zhou lifted a hand.

The Premier smiled enigmatically. "Who says he was not brought to justice?" She turned to Thad. "The Dagger has a message for you, Captain Severance."

Thad looked as confused as Ell felt. "For me, not Ell?"

"For you, Captain." She reached behind her and retrieved a case from the cart's lower shelf, then set it in front of her. "I believe you told her that you wanted Dent's head on a pike."

Ell had a funny feeling about where this was going.

"Dacina wanted to know if this would suffice."

With the flick of a well-manicured finger, the case went from opaque to transparent.

Katie's knees cracked hard against the underside of the table as she crab-walked backward in shock. "That's… that's…"

Ell finished for her. "Asher Dent's head."

TWENTY:
BEADED, NOT BRAIDED

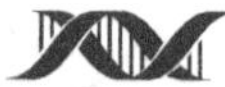

RECEIVING ROOM
STATE ASSEMBLY HOUSE
ERIDU, AKKADIA

"Well, you did tell her that," Ell commented, some weird sort of gallows humor bubbling up from inside her as she stared at the gruesome sight.

"I did not! I said I wanted him dismembered, his body spread to the four corners of the universe."

"You also suggested she gut him and jettison his entrails into Venus's atmosphere," Micah reminded him.

"No, *you* said that."

Pascal padded over to the table and took a careful sniff. *{Hmm. Smells like steak.}*

Katie grabbed him and hauled him back. "Ew, Pascal!"

Che leaned over to Rin Zhou. "This is what the Geminate call *camaraderie.*"

That shut them up fast.

"As for Dacina…" Che held something in his fisted hand. He

extended it to Ell. "She wanted me to give you this." He uncurled his fingers. Resting in his palm was a single red bead. "She says you earned it."

Ell lifted the bead from Che's hand and held it to the light. *One bead, one kill.*

"It will go well with the coloring of your hair," Rin Zhou said.

Ell shook her head. "I let the asshole live, though I'll probably regret it for the rest of my life."

Thad looked confused. "Why do I get the impression we're not talking about Dent any longer?"

"Ken. It was Ken who took that shot at you right before we entered the house. He was the one who gave us up to Dent, I'm sure of it." Ell's hand closed on the bead, then she held it out to Che. "I'm afraid I can't keep this."

But Che just stared back at her, amused, and refused to take it. "I see we are going to have to dispel this myth for you. Sad, for it has served us well for more than a century. The bead is not what marks an assassin. It is the braid." He closed Ell's hand over the bead once more. "Keep it. It is Dacina's way of claiming you as kin."

Ell stared back at Che, a mix of emotions swirling in her head. She realized it wasn't just this mission that was now complete, but also the mission that had started more than a year ago, around a different star altogether. A mission that began with a broken Unit operator, thrust into the unfamiliar role of NCIC agent. A mission that pitted Ell against a nameless, faceless assassin, chasing her halfway down the length of Hawking's McKendree cylinder. A more unlikely pairing, she could not imagine.

She looked down at the bead once more. "Truth is sometimes truly stranger than fiction," she murmured.

She felt Thad's hand on her shoulder.

"That it is, cher. That it is."

If you'd like to learn more about the actual science behind the fiction, turn to the Afterword. Perhaps the futuristic tech in this story isn't so far off after all!

BECAUSE ALL HEROES DESERVE AN ORIGIN STORY...

If you enjoyed Ell and Dacina's adventure and you haven't read about their first encounter, the first two chapters of *The Chiral Conspiracy* are appended to the end of this book.

And if you want to know exactly how creative Katie can be when she gets her hands on ActiveFiber, her origin story, *Operation Cobalt*, is available through all major booksellers.

FREE EBOOK OFFER

If you're curious how Ell lost her leg, that story is free to download as an ebook and is available on any device.

Use the camera on your mobile device or tablet to scan the QR code below. It will direct you to a page with links to all the major ebook retailers.

DAGGER'S EDGE: WHAT'S SCIENCE AND WHAT'S FICTION?

Shortly after completing the Chiral Agent trilogy, I fell into the habit of adding an afterword to all of my books, to share a peek behind the curtain at the science behind the fiction.

I do a lot of research when writing, and try hard to extrapolate believable tech based on real-world innovations happening today.

Some of it, admittedly, is more believable than others, but you might be surprised how often current theory parallels the fiction. Maybe some of the concepts contained in this story aren't as farfetched as you might think.

Read on to learn more about the science behind the Biogenesis Universe:

Can Venus be colonized?

Not in the traditional sense, no. At ground level, Venus is inhospitable. There's no getting around that. The atmospheric pressure on its surface is ninety-two times that of Earth—a crushing 1350 psi.

Its temperature can top 800°F/467°C. And it's corrosive. The planet is covered by thick clouds of sulfuric acid (so was Akkadia, if you recall, before they terraformed it).

Fifty kilometers above the surface, however, things change. Not the atmosphere; it's still toxic. But at this level, the temperature and pressure mimic that of Earth.

Geoffrey Landis, an aerospace engineer at of NASA has said, "At cloud-top level, Venus is the paradise planet." He proposes the use of aerostat habitats, habitats held up by floating balloons. This isn't as unrealistic as it might seem at first glance.

The air we breathe is a mix of nitrogen and oxygen. On Venus, it would be considered a 'lifting gas,' because it's lighter than Venus's own dense carbon dioxide atmosphere. This means that balloons filled with air would float on Venus, just like helium balloons (which are lighter than air) float here on Earth. They could also float the extra weight of a colony.

The atmosphere above the fifty-kilometer mark is comparable to ours, too. That means it's dense enough to provide protection both from galactic cosmic rays and the Sun's own emissions—solar flares and coronal mass ejections.

One interesting aspect of our sister world is its day/night cycle and its wind speeds. Considering the fact that one Venusian day is equal to 118 of ours, you would think colonists would be in for a three-month-long day and an equally long night.

Well, you'd be wrong.

The winds on Venus blow opposite its direction of rotation, and they blow fast. Top wind speed is 340 kilometers per hour (210 mph). Anything floating along in that jet stream is going to circle the planet once every four Earth days.

And why wouldn't they? A floating city would experience much less shear and structural stress if it quite literally 'went along with the flow.'

I'd gladly take a day/night cycle four times longer than ours over one that's three *months* long.

Can you envision a Venus covered by wall-to-wall aerostats? Wild, isn't it?

There are two major down sides that would have to be overcome, though. First, mining Venus is challenging, and not likely to be the best option. Importing material from Earth or asteroids would also be costly. And the material used to build aerostats is specific, at least for its outermost coating, to protect it from acid rain corrosion.

Venus made the news recently, too. A group of astronomers led by Jane Greaves from Cardiff University detected something that might be an indicator of life in its clouds.

They detected what's known as a spectral fingerprint—a light-based signature—of a gas called phosphine. MIT scientists have previously shown that if this were ever detected on a rocky planet, it could only be produced by a living organism. Kind of exciting, isn't it?

You can read more at:

https://www.planetary.org/articles/what-would-it-be-like-to-stand-on-the-surface-of-venus

and at:

https://news.mit.edu/2020/life-venus-phosphine-0914

Does audio chaff exist?

Nope, that's entirely fabricated. But speaking of fabric…

A silk fabric was just invented, barely thicker than a human hair, that is able to mute sound entirely. The fabric generates sound waves that interfere with an unwanted noise to cancel it out.

Here's the link, if you want to read about it:

https://www.masslive.com/news/2024/05/new-material-developed-by-mit-researchers-able-to-block-out-sound-entirely.html

What is Colloid Nano?

Colloids do exist. They're extremely tiny insoluble particles that are so light, they remain suspended in air.

Thanks to brownian motion, the force of the particles in the air around them is greater than the force of gravity attempting to pull them down, therefore they float and are susceptible to the activity of air currents.

In the Biogenesis Universe, I grafted nano onto them to create a noise-cancelling cloud, which obviously doesn't exist.

But who knows? Someday, in some not-so-distant future, someone might combine these two—colloids and noise-cancelling fabric— and invent audio chaff. Now, that would be amazing.

Can we print food?

We can now. That wasn't the case when I first wrote *The Chiral Agent* in 2020.

3D food printing made headlines in late 2023 when a creative machines lab at Columbia University printed a 3D vegan cheesecake, using 'inks' made from graham crackers, peanut butter, Nutella, banana puree, strawberry jam, cherry drizzle, and frosting. You can read all about that at this link: https://new.nsf.gov/science-matters/3d-food-printing-healthy-eating-delicious-desserts

The 3D printing mentioned in the Chiral Agent series draws from a different technology: the digital-to-biological converter, invented by Synthetic Genomics. In 2017, the privately held startup published a paper describing a fully automated, demand-based tabletop printer that could produce functional biologics from DNA sequence information.

Its creator, Craig Venter, understood the challenges of getting medicines from Earth to the Moon, or to Mars, in a timely fashion.

And the slow pace of rocket ships wasn't going to cut it. So why not print them on-site?

What if you had a DBC hooked up to your desktop computer? Venter asked himself. "We could email you insulin or a vaccine, and the device would produce it for you ready-to-go," he said.

And just like a printer needs cartridges, so does the DBC. But where a printer would use different colors of ink, a DBC would use chemicals instead. Pretty cool concept, huh?

Here's the link, if you want to read more about it: https://www.vice.com/en/article/craig-venters-digital-to-biological-converter-is-real/

ActiveFiber, and the difference between a colloid and a colloidene:

A colloidene is real, too. It is made from a colloid particle, but formed like single-layer graphene and patterned in a honeycomb lattice. It employs click-assembly techniques like those used in chemistry.

Click-assembly is the use of common codes, or chemical compounds—what we'd call building blocks—that are pre-loaded into 'bricks.' Pharmaceutical companies are using this kind of click chemistry to develop new cancer therapies.

The fiction comes when I turn this concept over, applying this chemical technique to nano. The result is a nanobot, programmed to rapidly alter existing nano to whatever the person controlling it needs it to be, as Katie loves to do with ActiveFiber.

I use ActiveFiber in ships like *Wraith* to allow its interior to quickly reform with respect to whatever direction is 'up' at the time. This is usually reserved for long flights when the ship is accelerating and generating an apparent gravity, or when the ship is docked and assumes the same gravity of the planet or space station where it is connected.

Thad and Task Force Blue also used ActiveFiber to prepare for Sam's rescue op in *Chiral Protocol.* The team constructed a

facsimile of the asteroid refinery where Sam was being held, then used it to conduct practice runs.

What's with the Chiral Pairs?

If by some remote chance, you picked up this book without reading the original trilogy, you might wonder about the quantum entanglement that gave Micah and Jonathan their unbreakable mental connection. And Pascal with Joule. And Snotface with Sneaky Pete.

Chirality isn't fiction, it's very much fact. Ask anyone who has taken a chemistry class. It's used extensively in pharmaceuticals, but also in materials science and agricultural chemistry.

The word 'chiral' is derived from the Greek word for 'hand.' It's used to describe the way a molecule is structured. Most, but not all, molecules have a 'handedness' to them that's determined by the way the molecule is structured. Some molecules have the exact same number and type of atom, but their molecular structure cannot be superimposed. In fact, if you were to look at the chemical formula, it would be apparent that they are mirror images of each other. In such a situation, the molecules are classified as chiral.

Chirality isn't excusive to chemistry, either. It is used in physics, where left- or right-handedness is used to describe the direction of a particle's spin. It can be found in electromagnetism and optics, where chirality can be applied to photoelectric devices and smart sensors.

Even your taste buds are chiral! It's well known that taste receptors are stimulated by ionic stimuli. That's what makes sodium chloride taste salty, or sugars sweet.

So, chiral molecules are real. The creation of a chiral organism, on the other hand, is entirely fiction, although I stuck with reality as much as I could.

I also did my best to capture the essence of what chirality means in a conversation I wrote between Micah and Sam in *The Chiral Agent*. As a refresher, here is an excerpt from that scene:

* * *

"This is a molecule," Sam said. "A connected group of different atoms. Building blocks of nature, right?"

Micah nodded.

She duplicated the molecule—and flipped it. The mirror images faced each other as they floated over the device, the atoms on the left now encircling the carbon atom in a reversed yellow, blue, red, white pattern.

"This is a chiral molecule. Each atom attached to the carbon atom in the center is assigned a priority. Going from the highest to the lowest, you'll travel around it in either a clockwise or counterclockwise direction. If you move clockwise, the molecule is right-handed. Counterclockwise, it's left-handed."

Sam's finger traced the paths along the two holographic figures as she spoke.

"Now, both molecules have the exact same physical properties—the same boiling and freezing points, the same densities, and so on. But they can react *very* differently with biologically active molecules."

She wiped the mirror molecules from the holo and replaced them with images of two plants. One was feathery and fernlike, the other had deep green oval leaves that looked almost furry.

She looked expectantly over at him. When it was clear he wasn't going to speak, she said, "What? Don't tell me you've never seen either of these plants before?"

Micah shook his head with a smile. "The one on the left looks like an herb. Dill, maybe? The other one… Sorry. Haven't a clue."

"Let me guess." Her tone turned dry. "You aren't the kind of guy who drinks the occasional mojito or mint julep."

He laughed. "Can't say that I do. Rather have a beer than anything fancy."

"Well, you're right. The one on the left is dill. The other one's mint. Both have a compound in them called carvone. The mint carvone has sweet notes to it and is right-handed. The dill one has savory notes and is left-handed. But other than that, their *physical* properties are identical."

He gave her a skeptical look. "You're telling me that just because they spiral one way and not the other, they taste different?"

"That's exactly what I'm saying."

"But…what's the big deal, then? Why would scientific research be so interested in something that just changes the way something tastes?"

"Because some of mirror compounds can be quite dangerous."

His eyes narrowed. "In what way?"

"It's well documented," she told him. "For example, one left-handed pharmaceutical that offers palliative effects has a mirror pair that causes deformities in human embryos. We learned centuries ago to be very careful with chiral direction."

Micah stared at her for a long moment, scratching the sleeping ferret in his lap idly as he contemplated her words.

"Okay, but, what does this have to do with me?"

She looked down, rubbing the tops of her thighs and gathering her thoughts.

"Bear with me for another minute, and I'll get to that, I promise. All life we've found so far in the galaxy is decidedly left-handed. And, although we've been able to synthesize right-handed molecules in the lab, science has been pretty spectacularly *unable* to get it to live outside the lab."

She looked back up at him, her eyes traveling over his face, sweeping down to his hands. Hands that were very much alive, cradling the ferret.

"Until now."

He followed her gaze down at the animal in his hands. "Until now?"

"A probe discovered naturally occurring chiral life on the planet deGrasse is orbiting. That's why the torus is here."

He blinked, processing the news. After a moment, he asked, "Okay. Why is that so important?"

She shrugged. "For some scientists, it's a sort of holy grail, I guess. They kept trying to find right-handed life that exists somewhere in nature, even knowing that if we did, it likely wouldn't be able to survive in our own ecosystems."

He looked up at that.

"Why not?"

"A chiral organism can only feed from its own kind," she explained. "Oh, it can digest a substance from its mirror-environment, but it gains no nutritional benefit from it. So right-handed life in a left-handed world would, in essence, starve."

Snotface began gnawing on Micah's thumb, interspersing it with small licks. He rearranged his hold on the ferret, but Snotface squirmed away, running up to his shoulder instead.

He stuck his nose in Micah's ear and snuffled. *{Sneaky Pete right-handed. So is Micah too.}*

The ferret's words seared their way through Micah's brain. The small creature couldn't have understood the implication of what he'd just said, could he? His head snapped up, his gaze seeking the doctor's.

"What did he mean by that?"

"He means we ended up with two problems on our hands," Harper interjected.

"We weren't just dealing with a traitor, out to get their hands on our chiral research," Sam said. "It turned out the Navy's chief scientist was running an illegal series of side experiments."

"Side experiments," Micah repeated, his gut tightening.

The voice inside his head. They'd done that. He caught and held Sam's gaze, a wary apprehension building inside him.

The truth. He needed it. Now.

Sam ran her hands up and down her thighs as if suddenly chilled. "Once we got here," she said, her words slow and deliberate, "we realized he'd been creating chiral clones of complex, multicellular organisms. Mice, ferrets. Larger animals, like the panthers."

Her eyes met his. He read pain there, mixed with an inexplicable guilt.

"And then he began to experiment on humans."

She stood, reached past him, and opened a cabinet. He heard the rustling of a wrapper, and when she returned to her seat across from him, a candy was in her hands. She held the mint out to him.

"Go ahead, captain." Her voice was a mix of sadness and curiosity. "Taste it."

He reached for the mint, unwrapped it and popped it into his mouth. And immediately spat it back out.

"What the hell?"

Her eyes met his steadily. "It tasted like dill, didn't it."

The burst of flavor, sharp, savory, still clung to his tongue.

"This is some sort of sick joke—"

"Captain," she interrupted, one hand reaching out to land on his knee, "the person in your cargo hold…"

He looked up sharply. "The one who looks like me."

"You have to understand, Captain." He was drowning in the guilt he saw in her eyes. "I took an oath. I couldn't let them kill you. And I couldn't let him die."

Dropping his hands to the bench, he gripped the edge tightly, until it cut into his palms, the pain grounding him in reality. "He's… the original, isn't he?"

She nodded, the guilt in her eyes morphing into a sympathetic pain.

"And what does that make me?"

Her hand tightened on his knee.

"Micah Case's chiral clone."

The rest is pure fiction.

Below are a few fictional 'definitions' for you. There is truth buried in here, but it's pieced together in a way that is neither logical nor attainable.

For instance, if you were to research Ricci-flat manifolds or Casimir energy or evanescent modes, you would find that they do exist—just not in the ways imagined in this series.

Calabi-Yau Gate – This method of folding space is powered by siphoning dark matter out of a Ricci-flat manifold. The manifold, a special curvature within the Bulk, is a place where the vacuum energy of space can be accessed. Once converted to Casimir energy, it is then used to bend the Bulk, allowing for instantaneous travel from one location in normal spacetime to another, regardless of distance. The amount of Casimir energy differs, based on the amount and direction of the bend.

Drakeskin stealth suit – A drakeskin suit with a nanoweave embedded into the topmost layer of fabric that is tunable to the environment, providing visible-spectrum stealth. The underlayers are made of metamaterials, which use transformation optics to shield the wearer from view by controlling electromagnetic radiation and guiding incident waves around the wearer.

Evanescent (E-V) Wire – E-V nanocircuitry is the core communication unit embedded in the brain. It makes use of the optical phenomenon of evanescent modes with imaginary wave numbers and a poynting vector of zero to achieve the mathematical equivalent of quantum tunneling for the instantaneous transmission of information.

LockPiks – An app every member of the Special Reconnaissance Unit has installed in the data partition of their military implant. A

LockPik works to subvert a lock's program while maintaining its program integrity so that it can be reset back to original specs after the LockPik's use.

Starshot Buoys and Ford-Svaiter nodes – F-S nodes use the concept of focusing vacuum fluctuations with parabolic mirrors to induce a quantized field wherein evanescent nanocircuitry can be used to establish instantaneous communication. An F-S node is encased inside a Starshot Buoy. Buoys are seeded throughout a star system in a pattern known as the Starshot Constellation. All inhabited star systems have deployed Constellations.

Scharnhorst Drive – Interstellar drive that generates a Casimir bubble. This allows the drive to both harness and magnify the Scharnhorst effect, a phenomenon in which light travels faster than c. The drive allows a ship inside its bubble to travel at triple the speed of light.

SmartCarbyne Nanofloss – This adaptation of SmartCarbyne is a lattice of ultrafine SC filaments, implanted to reinforce bone, muscle, and sinew. This military augmentation is usually given to fighter pilots and special operations soldiers.

It was originally adapted for military use to protect pilots in high-g maneuvers. An accelerometer embedded in the pilot's wire controls the deployment of an SC lattice, woven into the soft tissues of vital organs. When experiencing acceleration greater than what the human body can withstand, the SC lattice automatically hardens, protecting the pilot.

Tau-Neu Chambers – Stasis chambers where all atomic function is held in suspension. The term comes from the Latin symbol, tau, [τ] which in physics and engineering represents the time constant. Neu, or the Latin 'nu', represents the molecular vibration mode, v_x which, in stasis, is zero.

PRINCIPAL CHARACTERS

Dacina, The Dagger: Dacina is a member of the **Junxun Tèzhŏng,** Akkadia's elite intelligence branch of the State Army. Those chosen as Tèzhŏng are sent through a crucible of deep indoctrination that refines its members into surgically efficient killing machines.

Most Tèzhŏng operatives focus on a specialty, with the most elite being its assassins, like Dacina.

Elodie Cyr: Ell formerly served as a sergeant with the Geminate Alliance's Special Reconnaissance Unit. As a member of SRU Team Five, she held the position of sniper and overwatch. After her injuries, sustained during a covert operation to retrieve members of a consulate stationed at a habitat in the Sargon Straits, Ell was recruited by Agent Gabriel Alvarez to join the Navy's Criminal Investigation Command as a special agent.

Ell's first encounter with Dacina in *The Chiral Conspiracy* thrust her back into the world of special operations, and back into the lives of her former teammates.

Coalition of Worlds – The Coalition isn't a governing body, but rather an alliance of independent star nations, for the advancement of peace and collaboration between the settled worlds. Its members include the Sol, Alpha Centauri, and Proxima Centauri star systems.

Sol's member nations are Terra, Mars, Venus, and the Ganymede and Europa colonies. Alpha Centauri B's star nation is Zoser. Alpha Centauri A (Rigel Kentaurus) is the Akkadian Empire. Proxima Centauri's member nation is the Shang dynasty.

The Coalition's articles state that all eight governmental bodies are equally represented, however, some are unofficially regarded

as more equal than others.
The star nations within the Sol System hold the lion's share of influence.

WEAPONRY

CUSP – Compact Ultra-Short Pulse pistol uses a pulsed, laser-induced plasma to either paralyze, flash-bang, flash-blind, or deliver searing pain, depending on the weapon's setting.

P-SCAR – Pulsed Special Combat Assault Rifle.

Ziptie – a nano breach application for use in restraining people. Once placed onto exposed flesh, the app immediately unpacks itself, blocking an individual's wire from transmitting a call for help, and rendering the victim temporarily immobile.

Drakeskin stealth suit – A carbyne-reinforced synthsilk suit used by special operations forces when infiltrating hostile territory. It has a nanoweave embedded into the topmost layer of fabric that is tunable to the environment, providing visible-spectrum stealth.
The underlayers are made of metamaterials, which use transformation optics to shield the wearer from view by controlling electromagnetic radiation and guiding incident waves around the wearer.

PREVIEW: THE CHIRAL CONSPIRACY

ONE

Pirate Station
Straits of Sargon,
Akkadia
(Alpha Centauri A)

THE PIRATE STATION smelled like old socks.

Correction, NCIC Special Agent Elodie Cyr thought. *Old socks, worn throughout Hell Walk at the end of Recon.*

She'd become inured to such smells during active duty, first as a Marine, and then later when she joined the Navy's special forces. She'd left the Special Recon Unit four years ago to pursue a career with Navy Criminal Investigation Command, but some things just stuck with you.

Even when you'd rather they not, Ell thought, stifling a sigh.

Her previous life was also responsible for her current situation. She'd been taken hostage with three others, and was now trapped inside an ancient space station with an enviro system that should have been red-tagged before she was born.

The cuffs around her wrists looked like they'd been forged in a prior century, too, but they did the job. The Ziptie nanopackage they'd slapped on her neck before shoving her inside the holding area did the rest. The app blocked the wire in her brain, cutting off all comm and network access.

On the plus side, she could still walk and talk.

The Zipties they'd used back in the Unit were far more robust. They infiltrated body mods, rendering them inoperable. They also seized control of the SmartCarbyne lattice that reinforced most spacers' bodies, imposing paralysis.

The pirates should have gone for the more comprehensive version, but they hadn't wanted to lug their prisoners' inert bodies around. If Ell had anything to say about it, their laziness was going to cost them.

She had a stash of breach nanobots tucked in the shaft of her left boot, but with her hands behind her back, she'd have to be a contortionist to reach them. Still, it was worth a try.

She shifted, and the guard's attention snapped to her.

"Don't move," he warned.

"Just trying to get more comfortable." She kept her voice even, but continued tucking her legs under her.

"Legs straight, now!" he barked, jabbing the service end of his combat rifle at her, and she froze.

"Okay, okay," she said, extending them back out. "We're good."

The guard frowned at her, but didn't respond. He seemed impossibly young, with a face that looked as if it had never seen stubble.

The hard look in his eyes told her he was well aware of the impression he made, and was determined to overcome what he saw as the stigma of youth.

In the Unit, we would have taught him how to cultivate that misconception and use it to his advantage.

She shook the thought off, resuming her slow perusal of the room. There wasn't much here that could be used to subdue the guard, but that didn't stop her from studying its confines.

Her focus shifted abruptly when she felt a faint nudge against her shoulder. She kept her eyes trained on the baby-faced guard while she let herself lean against her fellow prisoner.

Fingers brushed against her wrist, followed by the sharp scrape of metal as a piece of wire tapped against her palm. Her expression remained unchanged, but she felt a flush of satisfaction as she wrapped her fingers around it.

Well done, Quinn, she thought.

Charles Quinn was still junior enough to be called 'probie,' though Ell didn't. The NCIC office on Hawking was understaffed at the moment, so it was just the two of them, and he didn't need the hazing.

Besides, she'd take one Quinn over three average workers any day. The man was resourceful, and had impressive recall.

This tiny scrap of wire was the perfect example. She'd mentioned her skill with ancient mechanical locks once in passing, but he'd obviously remembered it. Better yet, he looked for a way to take advantage of it.

As she bent the wire into two opposing ninety-degree angles, Quinn worked to distract the guard.

Nodding to the fourth person they'd taken prisoner, he asked, "Don't you think you should check on her? A hostage is no good to you if she's dead."

Ell's fingers traced the upper portion of the lock, gently easing the wire in and applying upward pressure. She felt the ratchet lift.

The guard glared at Quinn. "She's fine. Now shut up."

Holding the wire in place, Ell flexed her hand, pressing against the cuff. She felt the teeth begin to slowly slide through the opening.

"I don't see her breathing," Quinn's voice sounded doubtful. "Couldn't you at least scan her?"

The wire slipped. Ell relaxed her hand on an inhale, wiggling her fingers on the exhale. She tried again. Three more teeth slid through the ratchet and Ell palmed the wire while working her wrist free of the shackles.

"I said," the guard stepped closer, aiming his pulse rifle at Quinn's forehead. "Shut. The. Fuck. Up."

"He'll be quiet," Ell told the guard hastily, then leaned into Quinn, using the movement to reach her hand behind his back.

"Stand down."

He nodded and slumped slightly forward, the action a cover to give her better access to his bound wrists.

By the time she had Quinn freed, her shoulders ached. Ell sucked in a slow, deep breath and readied herself to do it all again—this time, to free the man on her right.

Quinn, miming still-bound hands, did what he could to draw attention from her. He cleared his throat. The pirate shot him a narrow-eyed look.

"Our people are coming. When they get here, shit's going down," Quinn said, his tone calm and level. "There's no way you're going to win this."

Before he could continue, the guard scoffed. "What, you think you're someone important? You're just a glorified cop, man."

Quinn's eyes narrowed. "NCIC still goes through basic and advanced, just like everyone else, kid. And then the real training begins."

That's it. Keep distracting him, Ell silently encouraged, as her shoulder made contact with the major seated to her right.

She and Rafe went way back. While she'd been with the Unit, Rafe Zander had flown Shadow Recon. He'd been responsible for hauling Ell's ass out of many a hot zone, back in the day.

Like her, he'd moved on. Unlike her, he'd stayed in the same Navy track. He'd risen to the rank of major, and now commanded an entire squadron.

To her left, Quinn tried a more persuasive tone.

"You know the Navy's looking for us. You have four naval personnel here." He shook his head. "If you let us go now, it'll go easier on you when they get here."

Using her fingers against his forearm, Ell quickly tapped out a code she knew Rafe would understand, one all Unit operators and Shadow Recon pilots knew. Within seconds, she felt his bound hands brush against hers, and she went to work.

The guard glowered at Quinn, waggling his pulse rifle threateningly. "Who's got the gun and who's trussed up tighter 'n cargo in a net, huh, asshole?"

Quinn walked a tightrope with the guard, alternately persuading and goading.

At times, Ell thought she should mentally rename Baby Face to Red Face. Just when she began to worry Quinn had provoked the guard too far, he backed off, only to begin again a few seconds later.

The technique was the perfect distraction.

Right up to the moment Rafe's shackles hit the ground with a soft *clang*.

What the—?

Ell's stomach plummeted, dismay stabbing through her at Rafe's unexpected clumsiness.

The guard broke off, shooting a suspicious look their way. Motioning to Ell and the major, he ordered, "Move away from each other. Slowly, now."

Ell moved toward Quinn, while Rafe shuffled in the opposite direction. He managed to make more noise with his cuffs, and Ell realized he was doing it to give her an opening.

Ell took it.

Using the man's momentary distraction, she launched her attack. With the flick of a wrist, her handcuffs went slicing through the air, a crude form of nunchaku.

Military-grade picosensors woven throughout her body kicked in as she exploded to her feet, boosting reflexes far beyond the human norm. Quinn and Rafe were right behind her.

Quinn dove for the weapon Ell's handcuffs had sent flying when they wrapped around the guard's wrist. Rafe raced for the downed specialist in the corner.

Ell drove her right shoulder into the guard's abdomen, hand crossing to wrap behind his opposing knee, jerking him off his feet. Instinctively, the guard tried to roll out from under her. She allowed him a half turn before grabbing his arm and forcing it forward.

Snaking one hand under his armpit and the other around his neck, she levered him into a bow and arrow choke hold.

His face already red from exertion, his eyes went wide when he realized his air supply had been cut off. He began to struggle, but then Quinn was there, the guard's rifle aimed unerringly at the man's face.

"Freeze," the investigator barked, and then shrugged with an evil grin. "Or don't. Your call."

Wisely, the young guard froze.

She released her hold about his neck and reached for the Ziptie hidden in the shaft of her boot, while Rafe used their discarded cuffs to bind the guard. She waved the nanopackage at the major before slapping it against the back of their prisoner's neck.

"He had plenty of opportunity to call for reinforcements before I ziptied him," she warned Rafe.

He shook his head. "He didn't." The major jerked his chin at the guard. "Look at his face. It never even occurred to him to call for help."

Ell glanced down at the guard and realized Rafe was right. The guard's face had reddened once more, only this time in embarrassment at the major's words.

The look in his eyes—about the only expressive thing allowed him under the influence of Ell's more comprehensive Ziptie— clearly telegraphed his dismay.

Shaking her head, she gave Baby Face a pat on the cheek, and then rocked back on her heels. Careful not to cross Quinn's line of fire, she rolled to her feet.

Rafe shot her an unreadable look. "You ready to get out of here, Sarge?"

Ell couldn't quite hide her flinch at his use of her old rank, but she covered it by motioning to the fourth prisoner. "Okay, fine. I'll get the door. You grab her."

Rafe lifted a brow. "You forgotten the way we do things in the Navy? Last I recall, majors give sergeants orders, not the other way around."

Ell scowled at him. "I'm not a sergeant any longer," she reminded him. "You're combat; I'm NCIC."

"Ma'am, yes, ma'am," he said, amusement coloring his tone as he stepped toward their prone companion.

Narrowing her eyes, she stood there a moment, studying him. Rafe's actions weren't adding up. She wondered what side game he had going on that he wasn't telling her.

He shot her a knowing look, which told her exactly nothing other than he knew his actions had her mystified.

Ell shook her head, dismissing Rafe and turning to Quinn. She motioned for the door. "You know there is a good chance they have at least one more standing outside. They hear the door opening and they'll have weapons drawn before you can get a bead on them."

Quinn nodded, brows drawing together. "The thought had occurred to me," he admitted. "Got any suggestions?"

"Yeah," she drew the word out thoughtfully, playing out the scene in her mind.

Placing her hand over the door's control mechanism, she deposited a round of breaching nano into it. It synched with the software in her wire, showing her a lock that was easily a decade or more out of use.

"Okay," she murmured. "That'll be easy enough to pick."

She looked over her shoulder at Quinn and then Rafe, who had the fourth hostage hoisted over his shoulder in a fireman's carry.

"Stay clear of the door," she instructed Rafe, waving him over toward Quinn. "Quinn, open the door on my mark. Be prepared to back me up like you did when we took out Baby Face. Got it?"

Quinn nodded and both men stepped back against the bulkhead. Ell moved to the opposite side of the door, crouching low to the deck. "On three. One…two…"

Quinn triggered the door and Ell propelled herself up and into the guard who had turned at the sound. An *oof* sounded from the pirate as he landed on his back, his weapon clattering to the deck.

Peripheral vision told her Quinn had engaged another guard just as the man beneath her rolled. Ell barely escaped the fist that came crashing down toward her face, jerking her head to the left at the last moment.

She thrust her fist upward in what looked like a cross jab. The man's chin jerked back instinctively, but she wasn't going for the chin. Instead, she hooked her fingers around the bony scapula ridge that ran just behind the top of the man's shoulder and *pulled*. That action levered Ell up while propelling the man toward the deck.

The pirate was now face down with Ell on top. She reached for the pistol strapped to the man's right thigh, but the pirate tried to buck her off. Ell fought to put the man in a grappling hold but found herself suddenly airborne.

She landed against the bulkhead with a soft grunt just as she heard the click of a combat rifle and a low, guttural, "Freeze!"

Ell recognized that voice.

She looked up and saw familiar brown eyes, narrowed on the guard she'd been battling. The owner of those eyes gave her a quick look, his smile a brief slash of white against an ebony backdrop, before turning back to glare the pirate.

Thaddaeus Severance was a powerhouse of a Marine, as charismatic as he was strong. Ell had learned long ago she was defenseless against the captain's easy charm, so she wasn't surprised to find herself grinning back at him like an idiot.

The man had won her over the moment they'd first been introduced. Elodie had always hated her first name, had felt it far too flowery for a Marine. His first words had put paid to that.

"El-o-die," he'd rolled the word around in his mouth, his signature smile curving slowly about his lips. "Now that, there, is one badass name."

She'd thought he was hazing her…until he explained.

"Never met someone whose name spelled out what would happen if you messed with her." He'd shaken his head in admiration. "Elo-die. Hello-die. Sweetest combat name I ever heard."

Ell shook off the memory and rolled to her feet as Thad spoke.

The words, though clipped, were spoken in a distinctive and familiar twang as he tilted his head down to indicate his tactical vest. "Zipties, right pocket. Antidote code, left."

She nodded, reaching for the nanopackage that would restore

her wire access.

"Thought you needed rescuing, *ami*," he said in a low rumble only she could hear. "Glad to see my intel was wrong."

"I never say no to a helping hand," she murmured in reply, bending to slap the restraint on the guard Thad had pinned.

Thad gave a low "Oorah," and then snapped his rifle back out to cover the passageway.

Ell crossed to apply the Ziptie to the third guard before passing the antidote code to Rafe and Quinn.

As Ell scooped up the rifle that had gone flying when she first tackled the guard, Thad nudged the pirate. "C'mon *coo-yon*, get up."

Ell shot Thad a quick glance as she helped haul the pirate to his feet. "You alone, Captain?"

"Nope. Jack's with me, as are Asha and Boone."

Ell saw the look that Thad leveled at her when he mentioned those last two names.

Asha, the medic who'd kept her alive after the IED exploded, killing Mike, their teammate.

Boone, the man who had taken her place as the team's sniper, while doctors worked to rebuild her.

She managed to keep her expression neutral, but only just. Moments later, she saw the icon for a combat net pop up on her overlay.

{You're about to have company,} she heard Boone warn Thad as she joined. *{Headed your way.}*

Thad swore. *{How the hell did they know we'd sprung the prisoners?}* he demanded.

{Coincidence, maybe?} Jack's voice sounded doubtful. *{But they're inbound, half a klick aft of your position.}*

A map appeared, showing icons denoting friendlies in green, tangos in red. Five reds were converging on them from three different directions.

{That's no coincidence. Move out,} Thad ordered, gesturing them to follow. He turned and shot the major a questioning look. "Need help with that hostage, *ami*?"

Rafe shook his head. "I'm good. Lead on, Captain."

Ell fell into a run behind Thad as the big Marine raced toward the hatch and the Shadow Recon ship she knew awaited them. Quinn followed, Rafe bringing up the rear.

Five years, she thought. *It's been five years since I was last with the team. How the hell did I end up back here?*

TWO

GNS *WRAITH*
STRAITS OF SARGON
AKKADIA

WRAITH'S COCKPIT WAS tense and quiet, all four members of her crew focused on keeping the ship's tenuous connection to the pirate station hidden from its residents.

{Asha and I will flank them,} a voice came across the Marine combat net they were monitoring. *{We'll drive 'em to you Boone.}*

{Wait one,} a second voice interrupted, the voice of Boone, the team's sniper. *{Two more approaching. Patrol, coming up rim passageway, spinward side, in five.}*

A two-click acknowledgement followed.

Captain Jonathan Micah Case let the communication flow past him. Anything the Marines needed the ship's crew to know about could come through Yuki, his co-pilot.

Right now, Micah's world had shrunk to a single point, a feather-light connection between the Direct Action Penetrator Helios he commanded and the battered hatch the fast attack craft hovered beside.

The connection between the wire embedded inside his brain and the ship's SyntheticVision system was so deep, Micah couldn't have said where the ship ended and he began.

It was as if the ship wasn't even there. Or, rather, he *was* the ship.

He felt as if he could reach out and touch the accordioned surface of the tube snugged up against the dull silver of the station, though he didn't dare. At the moment, each gesture, even the slightest of hand movements, meant something more. His limbs were the ship's thrusters. Her sensors, his eyes.

Without this deep link, he never could have maintained the delicate balance required to keep an exit point open for the Marines and the hostages they'd been sent in to retrieve. He needed the advantage the SV link provided to remain in perfect sync with the small habitat as it rotated upon its central axis.

Wraith should have been able to lock in a velocity that matched the fusion plant driving the station's central axis, but the plant was old and poorly maintained. Its rate of rotation fluctuated just enough that it required Micah to ride it constantly.

A lesser pilot might find this challenging—but a lesser pilot would not be commanding a DAP Helios. Few could fly an attack craft of *Wraith*'s caliber; fewer still could operate her with such precision.

To a one, those pilots who could lay claim to such a distinction were members of the Alliance's elite Shadow Recon teams.

The sound of weapons fire coming across the combat net indicated the Marines had surprised a small group of pirates guarding the hostages.

{There goes our quiet ride out of here.} Yuki's voice was dry as her hands danced across the co-pilot's console, scanning for enemy spacecraft.

He'd caught the rhythm of the station's lumbering spin. Knowing a smooth patch was ahead, he chanced a quick glance past the station's curved hull to the dense ring of asteroids that lay between them and the gate at the Alpha Centauri system's heliopause.

Micah's mind made the rough calculations as his eyes returned to the umbilical before him. *Three AU and some change.*

His gaze focused briefly on the readout overlaid on his three-hundred-sixty-degree view. The Bravo Charlie that Thad had placed onto the hatch's external access pad still read green. The BC, or breaching canister, was programmed to send false signals back to the pirates' monitoring system to make it seem as if the hatch was still securely sealed.

That was good news. The pirates might know they had intruders, but they couldn't know yet exactly where they'd entered, though all entrances were now suspect. Hopefully, they'd be able to extract before the pirates had a chance to trace their location.

{Three down.} That was Jack, Thad's second.

{Make that four,} Asha called out. *{Last one's yours Cap.}*

{Got 'im,} Thad said.

On the heels of that came Boone again. *{Perimeter's clear.}*

No more words were said, but everyone aboard *Wraith* knew what would be coming next.

It was time to exfil.

Seconds later, the ship's open hatch filled with Marines in powered battle armor. Micah monitored both interior and exterior feeds as the first to arrive launched himself through the umbilical.

The man wrapped gauntleted fingers around a handhold, piking himself into the ship with economical movement. In an instant, he had reversed his position, bracing to receive the hostages.

It was then that Will noticed they had company.

{Two technicals just launched,} the flight engineer and crew chief sang out from the cradle behind Micah. Will pushed the feed to him with accompanying data that laid out the specs of each craft.

Both were improvised fighting vessels. One was a small cargo tug with a railgun bolted to its undercarriage; the other was an ancient comm-relay satellite that had been retrofitted with a pair of 5 mm lasers.

The speed at which they shot from the small station's shuttle bay belied their ungainly appearance. Turning in a tight arc, the noses of both crafts aimed for the open hatch.

Inside *Wraith*, the hostages were being pulled inside, one by one, Marines hot on their heels. The first Marine hauled Ell Cyr through the opening and then turned, his hand already extended to catch the next hostage. Ell braced on the other side of the hatch, assisting with the catch and urging the hostage to make a hole for the next person inbound.

Three seconds later, Micah heard a *{Go! Go! Go!}* as Thad sealed the end of the umbilical and pushed it away from the hatch.

{Maneuvering!} was all the warning Micah gave the team. He kicked the nose over, dipping down and away from the two vessels attempting to flank *Wraith* on both sides.

He spared a glance at an internal feed and was relieved to see Thad being hoisted into the ship. Boone reached past him to pull the umbilical in after he cleared the opening. Micah cut the feed when the ship registered full hull integrity, and returned his attention to the aggressors on his tail.

{Incoming,} Will warned, followed by a flash of tracer light that told him the tug's railgun had fired.

The cloud of drones surrounding *Wraith* were under Yuki's control; she'd disengaged their cloaking routine when the technical had showed, flipping them into a point-defense formation.

A pair of them broke off, reconfigured as electronic countermeasures. One of the Dazzlers began to emit decoy EM while the other jammed signals. Yuki engaged the rest of the drones in point-defense, their lasers chewing into the slugs the tug had tossed at them.

{Nina! Steel!} Micah began jinking the ship in an evasive pattern, and his gunner responded instantly. She'd had the two pirate ships centered in the reticle of her RAU-19 triple-barrel railgun ever since Will had identified the tangoes. Now, she went weapons free.

Micah felt the vibration through his deep connection with the ship, heard the small *foomp-foomp* of the railgun as it returned fire. The tug tried to evade but it wasn't built for maneuverability, its makers never envisioning it going head-to-head with a DAP Helios.

The steel rounds slammed into the tug just aft of its tiny cockpit.

Though better armored than most tugs, it was no match for the projectiles' closing velocity, and the slugs tore into the small vessel's hide as if it were tissue paper.

The RAU spat another short burst of fire to finish the tug off just as Micah tweaked the ship's thrusters to avoid a laser shot from the converted satellite. Nina reacquired the satellite and took the shot at the same time Yuki unleashed laser fire from point defense to chase down *Wraith*'s wild slugs and incinerate them.

His co-pilot's action was automatic. Once a slug was fired in space, it kept going until it found an object with enough stopping power to arrest its velocity. That might be a non-issue if it ended up impacting an asteroid, but it could just as easily hit an innocent vessel, a mining platform, or a space habitat.

Leaving ballistic ammunition shooting through a populated system was the kind of thing only terrorists and pirates did. Cleanup laser fire went part and parcel with good trigger discipline. If Yuki had been too busy to address it, *Wraith*'s SI would have released a cleanup drone to address the matter.

Tug out of commission, Micah twisted the Helios and Nina let fly a twenty-kilogram tungsten sabot that punctured the center of the satellite and continued through, embedding itself into the pirate station's flank.

Sparks flew from the satellite as its two jury-rigged lasers exploded, the fiery bloom a sharp, attenuated thing, as explosions in a vacuum tended to be.

{Shit! Tacticals were just a diversion, folks.} Will's exclamation was accompanied by the wailing of *Wraith*'s proximity alarms as Micah spotted a salvo of smart missiles appear from behind the station.

He ducked. Connected as he was to *Wraith*, the ship followed suit. The oncoming missiles did as well, their onboard computers compensating for every course adjustment he made.

{Dazzlers,} he called to Yuki. The thought barely had time to form before a full dozen additional drones came shooting out from *Wraith*'s hold.

Had he not known they were there, he might have missed them. Their sensor cross-section was almost indistinguishable until they reached the envelope—and then they lit up, smothering the missiles in a cacophony of EM.

The missiles lost lock on *Wraith*. He saw their noses wobble and dip, seeking the strongest signal that matched the Helios they'd been programmed to strike.

There were too many points in space broadcasting that identical signature; to a one, the missiles turned, locking onto the nearest drone. The impacts were impressive, successive detonations, one after the other, immolating both missile and Dazzler alike.

{Heads up!} Will's voice held a warning. *{Time for the main attraction.}*

The flight engineer's comment was followed by a stream of data detailing weapons load-out as two Akkadian Hydra Mark V fighters, bristling with armament, appeared from behind the curve of the station. *Wraith*'s SI pinged a warning, letting Micah and the rest know the vessel had already acquired a targeting lock.

The SI responded first, sending the ship into a series of complex twists faster than even Micah's augmented pilot's reaction time could match.

He joined in, mixing his own moves with the more predictable computer-generated evasions as laser pulses lanced toward them from the Hydras. He threw *Wraith* into a helical turn, pulling her up abruptly, only to whip her over onto her side in a blindingly fast move.

He did it again and again, corkscrewing through the black in a series of increasingly complex and unpredictable moves, while Yuki and Nina hammered at the attacking vessels.

The Dazzlers weren't as effective when pitted against human-augmented SIs, so Yuki deployed them as auxiliary weapons platforms, harrying the fighters, using their agility and maneuverability to eat away at the enemy's defenses.

Nina managed to sever the fuel feed on one of the Hydra's fusion drives and its accel drop was instantaneous. Micah spared it a look as its pilot veered off at a constant velocity it now had no way of stopping, but that moment of distraction cost him.

The second ship scored a hit on *Wraith*'s flank. The laser bit into the ship's ablative surface, the impacts searing like a hot poker against unprotected skin, before dispersing.

Micah ignored it. He'd long ago grown used to the sympathetic echo of pain that skipped along his neural interface before the SyntheticVision system could dampen it. Quickly enough, it faded, the shot's kinetic and heat energy dispersing through the Helios's picofoam interlayer with minimal effect to the craft.

Twice more, Micah dipped and twisted, thrusters firing in a mad and drunken dance, until one last tungsten salvo ripped through the remaining Hydra's shadow shield, its fusion plant's safety interlocks sending it into automatic shutdown.

"Nice job," he heard, just as a firm hand clapped down on his shoulder and the simulation ceased. The pirate station morphed into a decommissioned destroyer, pulled from a boneyard and towed into place.

The fictional Alpha Centauri gate disappeared off his sensors, to be replaced by a Military Operations Area adjacent to the Hawking habitat, in orbit around Procyon's F-class star, Merki.

The Hydras resolved into a pair of Alliance Novastrike fighters, and the tacticals turned back into standard targeting drones, used for warfare simulations and live-fire test runs when the MOA was active.

Awareness of his physical surroundings inside the ship also returned. As usual, it took a few additional seconds for Micah to extract himself from *Wraith*'s SyntheticVision feed. The sensation felt a bit like surfacing from a deep, crystalline pool.

He shook his head and blinked, eyes refocusing on the man standing between the two pilots' cradles. Rafe Zander grinned down at him, his expression one of mild envy.

"I miss that, you know," he told Micah, his eyes drifting meaningfully to the SV control panel.

Micah quirked a smile, dipping his head in a brief nod of

acknowledgement. "Want a rematch? I'll give up the pilot's seat and play hostage this time."

Zander shook his head, a wry twist playing about his lips. "Tempting, but you've traumatized my people enough for one day, Captain. They're a regular Navy squadron, not Shadow Recon, like us." He paused, then corrected, "Like you."

* * *

Ell heard the wistfulness buried in Rafe's tone, and wondered why the man had left Shadow Recon when he so clearly loved it.

We all have our stories, our private reasons.

She heard Thad's derisive snort as he started toward the pilot's cradle.

"All due respect, Major, that's bullshit, and you know it," Thad called out, having clearly heard the exchange. "Once SRU, always SRU, *ami*. The Unit never turns its back on its own."

The Marine had clipped his harness to *Wraith*'s frame just inside the ship's hatch while Micah sent the Helios spinning like a dervish. Exercise complete, he waded past the rest of his team—and those tapped to play hostage like Ell and Quinn—to debrief with Rafe.

The major turned. "Thaddaeus Severance the Third," he intoned, shooting Ell a wink. "Name like that belongs to a rich playboy living it up at the Royal Ganymede, not with some thick-necked jarhead out in space, busting heads together."

Thad grunted, spearing Rafe with a narrow, one-eyed squint. "Don' you be gettin' on my last nerve, there, hoss, or I might just have to forget that a Marine captain doesn't clean a major's clock at poker when we get back to the base tonight."

Anyone could tell the ribbing Rafe was handing out was a running joke between the two. Ell happened to know it dated back to when Rafe captained his own DAP Helios.

He'd inserted SRU Team Five into some of the more dangerous sectors of settled space on more than one occasion. Back then, Thad had been a sergeant, just like Ell.

Rafe had changed jobs. Thad had moved on to captain his own team.

Movement had her looking across the ship to where Boone sat, on the bench opposite hers. His eyes captured hers, darkening as he raised his brows in a silent question: *you okay?*

She smiled and nodded, knowing he saw past the lie. He knew, better than anyone, what she'd given up when she left and he'd taken up her mantle.

Being a sniper for the Unit was more than being a sharpshooter. There were an equal number of missions where the sniper played the role of overwatch, as was the case today.

It was the edge of the spear. It was exhilarating.

It was also where she'd been unable to stop her teammate from triggering an IED that caused explosive decompression, blasting Mike out the jagged hole of a habitat service hatch before she could reach him.

Thad's gauntleted hand had been the only thing that kept her from meeting that same fate. He'd pulled her back, carried her to the ship where Asha triaged her ruined leg, severed above the knee by a jagged metal spar.

Rafe's voice jolted her from her memories. She blinked, breaking eye contact with Boone and letting the reassuring pressure of Quinn's shoulder beside her anchor her to the present.

Looking toward the cockpit, she played back Rafe's last words in her head.

"By the way, how soon do they need you back on Ceriba?" he'd asked the Helios pilot.

She saw Micah shoot Yuki a glance, but his co-pilot just shrugged.

"Got a mission for us, Major?" Micah inquired.

Rafe shook his head. "More like a favor, really. The brass contacted me this morning, asked if we could route a civilian contractor to a secured location," he explained. "The guy's attending some symposium here in Midland."

Midland was Hawking's second largest city, located in the

middle of its four-thousand-kilometer-long span. It was a quick, half-hour shuttle hop away, from Portsmouth to the Midway docking ring.

Micah nodded slowly. "I'd have to clear it with Major Snell back on Humbolt, but I don't see a problem. Where's he need to go?"

"It's on your way. Well, close enough, at any rate," Rafe amended, causing Ell to wonder what secured location he was talking about. "I'll send you the coordinates. It'd save one of my pilots the round trip."

Micah shrugged. "If the major says it's okay, then sure, why not? I suppose the guy's used to military transport, if he's working for the Navy. When do we need to leave?"

Rafe thought a moment. "Sometime tomorrow or the next day should be fine. They've recalled him, but they didn't say anything about it being urgent." He paused. "Of course, that could change. You know how it goes."

Micah grunted but didn't otherwise comment on Rafe's vague response. They all knew how these things worked.

Rafe grinned abruptly, straightening. His gaze swept the ship, encompassing Thad's team and the flight crew.

Slapping a hand on the back of Micah's chair, he added, "Which means…." His eyes lit briefly on Ell, laughter dancing in their depths. "There's plenty of time for the Marines and Shadow Recon to pay up. You guys owe my Navy crew a round of drinks."

"Now, hold on there, *ami*." Thad folded his arms and lowered his head, shooting the major a one-eyed glower.

Rafe's brow rose. "The bet was that you couldn't get in and out undetected." He leveled a finger at the Unit leader. "My people detected you."

Just like that, everything snapped into place with crystal clarity.

"That's because you gave us up to them!" Ell cut in accusingly, shouldering her way forward. "The handcuffs. The fact they knew we'd escaped. You were a ringer!"

Rafe grinned at her, his gaze flipping from Ell, to Micah, and then back to Thad. "All's fair in war, folks. I never said the pirates wouldn't have a plant hanging back with the hostages, now did I?"

Ell saw Micah stifle a grin as Thad stood glowering at the major before shaking his head and stomping aft.

"Damned fuckin' pissant Navy pilots," they heard him mutter, the words a cadence matching his every step.

"Oooh-rah," she heard Rafe murmur under his breath, eyes pinned to Thad's retreating back. "Gotcha."

Thank you for reading this preview!

The Chiral Conspiracy is available to order through all major booksellers.

ACKNOWLEDGMENTS

There are several people I want to thank, who help me to bring my very best to you with each endeavor.

I've said it before and I will say it again; a good editor can turn a good manuscript into a great one. This tale would not be nearly as clean or easy to read without the help of Scott Walker. Thanks does not begin to express my appreciation.

It's a rare gift to have experts in the field that an author can count on for advice, especially when one strays into areas of science they know nothing about. I owe John A. a huge debt of thanks for lending me his expertise.

Marti, as always, you find the tiniest errors, and I'm forever grateful for that.

And Rob, thank you for spurring me on to finish this last story and complete the final arc.

Lastly, I want to thank you, my readers, for waiting nearly four long years for the final chapter in the Chiral trilogy, the door I left open on Asher Dent. I hope his demise was satisfying—and one worth the wait.

Fair skies and tailwinds,
L.L. Richman

August, 2024

ALSO BY LL RICHMAN

For updates on upcoming titles see https://www.llrichman.com

The Biogenesis War

> The Chiral Agent, June 2020
>
> The Chiral Protocol, September 2020
>
> Chiral Justice, February 2021
>
> Dagger's Edge, September 2024

The Biogenesis War Files: The Early Years

> Operation Cobalt, December 2020
>
> Ambush in the Sargon Straits, June 2020
>
> The Chiral Conspiracy, June 2020
>
> Sudden Death, August 2021

Vision Rising

> Vision Rising, May 2023
>
> Vision's Gambit, June 2023
>
> Vision's Pawn, July 2023

Battlefield Diplomacy

> Battlefield Diplomacy, Winter 2024
>
> Lost Colony, Winter 2024
>
> Insurrection, Early 2025

RIFT (A Near-Future Technothriller)

> Rift, Early 2025
>
> Splintered, Mid 2025

Enfield Genesis

Alpha Centauri: Rise of the Kentaurus AIs, 2018

Proxima Centauri: Hunt for the Lost AIs, 2018

Tau Ceti: The Phage, 2018

Epsilon Eridani: Crisis in the Little River, 2019

Sirius: Flight of the Hyperion, 2019

The Sol Dissolution Series (with M. D. Cooper)

Venusian Uprising, 2019

Assault on Sedna, 2020

Hyperion War, 2020

The Fall of Terra, 2021

ABOUT THE AUTHOR

L.L. Richman has a diverse career background, having spent more than a decade working in radiation physics, and twice that as a director of film and video. An avid pilot and photographer, Richman has close ties to the special forces community and can often be found flying a Piper Cherokee.

DON'T MISS A THING!

Connecting with you as a reader is one of the most rewarding things about writing. For more information on upcoming releases or the latest news on space science and technology, use the QR code or this link https://www.llrichman.com/newsletter/ to subscribe to the newsletter.

If you're active on Facebook, join the Spacetime Speakeasy with LL Richman. There, you'll get some behind-the-scenes intel on the science used in the books, plus some really bad dad jokes.

You can get to the Speakeasy by using the QR code below, or by following this link: bit.ly/SpacetimeSpeakeasy.